NO REASON ON EARTH

NO REASON
ON EARTH

A Short Story Collection by

Katharine Haake

Dragon Gate, Inc.

PORT TOWNSEND / SEATTLE

WASHINGTON

c.2

Grateful acknowledgment is made to the following publications in which some of these stories first appeared: *The Minnesota Review*, "Another Kind of Nostalgia"; *The Greensboro Review*, "Bear and Other Pale Giants"; *Telescope*, "Recently I've Discovered My Mistake"; *New England Review* and *Bread Loaf Quarterly: Writers in the Nuclear Age*, "The Meaning of Their Names"; and *Indiana Review*, "Burning the Lost Country."

Dragon Gate, Inc. and the author wish to express their gratitude to the Literature Program of the National Endowment for the Arts for a grant that helped support the publication of this book.

Designed by Tree Swenson.
The type is Palatino.
Cover art is from a watercolor painting, "This – Way," by Alan Clark.

Dragon Gate, Inc., 508 Lincoln Street
Port Townsend, Washington 98368

Library of Congress Cataloging in Publication Data

Haake, Katharine.
    No reason on earth.

    Contents: Another kind of nostalgia – One pair red, one pair blue – Bear and other pale giants – [etc.]
    I. Title.
PS3558.A145N6   1986   813'.54   86-2004
ISBN 0-937872-32-6
ISBN 0-937872-33-4 (pbk.)

CONTENTS

FOR MY PARENTS

It is not down in any map; true places never are.

Chapter xii, *Moby Dick* by Herman Melville

Another Kind of Nostalgia

I. THEO AND FRANK

THEO'S husband, Frank, was a drop-in center counselor; Theo was a drop-in center bride. Now at the height of post-pseudoradical, liberal affectation, Frank wants to dispel all notion that their coupling was unethical.

"I loved her," he tells his brother, Billy. "I still do."

Billy says nothing.

IN RETROSPECT, Theo's not so certain she wasn't a tiny bit taken advantage of, but Theo's had more than a decade to obscure the way she felt when they first married. Nor do I hold that against her, inclined as I am to believe that having made it to the eighties we're all a little anxious (never mind our protestations) to forget how we were in the sixties. Take Theo, for example, who at sixteen ran away from a small town in Nebraska, sold flowers back and forth across the country, strung herself out on drugs, marched against the war, and came to love both sexes before finally ending up three years later in another small town, this one in northern California, at a funky halfway house where one of the counselors had the bluest eyes and a particular way with his guitar which, taken together at once, lured Theo off the streets and into his bed in a single night.

That's in the far north part of California not many people know about—up there where you have your red hills, you have your dams and artificial lakes. You also have your farming, your ranching, your lumber industry. I'm fond of the valley myself, and its endless lonesome towns, mosquito-infested all summer, with the main street Foster Freeze still featuring hand-dipped cones and the heavy cannery breezes lingering sweetest at dawn, at dusk. They have a certain almost musty quality, those towns, a feel over things as if out of the past. More recently, there's been an exodus of southern urbanites, tired of the way they've been living. It's an old story; like attracts like and nothing is ever the same. I'm not being bitter, I'm just trying to explain why when Theo's last ride dropped her off on Interstate 5 there was somewhere she could go to crash, and why when six years later Frank left social service to invest in coffee beans, his business success was guaranteed.

Sometime between the one event and the other, Theo and Frank were married. The wedding took place in the same room where they'd met. Theo wore bright grosgrain ribbons in her hair to match the rainbows on the wall and she went barefoot, though it was February. Frank played his guitar. Theo danced. Frank said some poems. When it was over, Theo was tired but she made love with her new husband anyway, as she did in those days every night, both pre- and post-maritally, not to mention mornings, afternoons, between staff meetings, and before and after sessions, all the time. This physical extravagance continued, altogether, for about three years—right up to the time Theo's first pregnancy ended in abortion and abruptly, unexpectedly, their intimacies ceased.

"THAT was not a good time for either of us," Frank tells Billy. "I was level-headed, logical. Theo had nightmares."

Billy, who knows all about nightmares, nods in that bobbing manner of his, face slightly turned away because of the scars.

"SCREW your clients if you're horny," Theo told Frank when their troubles started. "I can't bear it."

And though Frank had been discreet, Frank had done what she said. In this way, their marriage, never easy, survived to a second period of ripeness at the end of its fourth year. Frank, who delights even now in the memory, refers to this time as their *sexual renaissance*.

"SHE was different," he tells Billy. "What you might call randy. Always ready for it, always hot."

Billy, for reasons unrelated to his brother, feels himself getting hard.

FRANK'S right about Theo: she *was* different then. For her, though no cause was apparent, it was as if all the grief that lay between the present and Nebraska — for now she'd come to think of so much of what had happened as fraught with grief — had suddenly dispersed, uncovering in its absence somewhere inside her older self her adolescent body. This was not something she had anticipated, not even hoped or longed for, just that one morning (it was September, you could smell apples and the smoke of rice stubble burning down the valley) she woke to discover that during the night she had thrown off the sheets and rent her long cotton gown. But it didn't feel like after a nightmare. The sun through the east window made warm patterns of light on her body. She turned her face to it, slipped out of her gown and touched herself, gingerly at first, then more experimentally. Nothing bad happened. It was all right. Theo began to explore in earnest, and as she was exploring, she remembered the cornfields where she had played as a girl. Soon her hands on her nipples, her thighs were as quick and rough as corn husks in the wind. After awhile, she roused Frank and forced his bearded face over the same ground. Frank, taken by surprise, did not once think of corn, but though their minds followed different paths, their bodies found the same one and this went on for months.

Not that Frank didn't have his doubts. A man, just like a woman, does. A man has doubts. And they know each other, these two, not merely as husband and wife do, but with an instinct, uncanny and precise. Frank knows, for example, perhaps better than Theo does herself, that his wife's strongest impulse is to bear children and nurture and raise them. He has known this all along, from the first night she showed up and he had to use a condom because she laughed and said, "What the hell, I take my chances. I leave these things to God." Whereas Frank prefers to leave God out of things. You could say, then, that he is analytical and Theo more intuitive. You'd almost have to say that as, sadly, his aversion to procreation is almost as intense as her desire for it. Hence the abortion, though Frank had intimations beforehand about the repercussions. It was, he insisted, unfortunate but necessary. Now, when the issue came up again, he tried once more to reason with her.

"Our chromosomes," he told her, "just think of what we've done to them. We'd have a goon. I can't believe even you would want a goon."

Theo, distrustful of science, would take a goon if it came to that and said so.

Frank played on her fears. "The world's on the brink of disaster. Could you really bring a child into this? Could you bear a child only to see that child blown to smithereens in a nuclear holocaust, in *the* nuclear holocaust?"

"Having children," Theo said, "is an act of faith, like any

other. Not having them is a greater assurance of our eventual annihilation than all the rest together. Do you know what I mean?"

Frank didn't. He put her off. "Ask me in another year."

"I'll be a year older in another year. I won't feel the same, but you will. You're just putting me off."

But Frank didn't put her off enough, couldn't, finally, because short of going back to condoms, which in encroaching middle age distressed him, and under the influence of his wife's transformation, he found himself powerless to circumvent her deception and intercept her second conception.

"THERE was nothing I could do," he tells Billy. "She was rabid. She was like a nymphomaniac with a new IUD, only without the protection. Every place I touched her made her come, and she made me touch her. What she wore — she wore these loose, sheer shifts and nothing underneath. During time-outs in televised ball games she sat naked on my lap. She dropped in at the drop-in center and, while Peter slit his wrists downstairs, made love to me in the office."

Billy, who has slit his wrists himself not once but many times, is suddenly uncomfortable with this conversation. He would like very much to change the subject but is afraid if he interrupts the natural course of things his stutter will return. And because he has fought almost all his life against it, he wisely does not want to bring it back, for then it might stay with him for good. So Billy resolutely remains silent.

WHEN Theo did conceive this time, Frank felt not betrayed or defeated so much as subject to a certain fate, long since determined without him. As there seemed nothing for it, he gave himself up to what he believed were the inevitable consequences. Morning after morning, blooming, beatific, Theo sipped her fresh-squeezed juice with a little inward smile, while across the breakfast table, hunched over shredded wheat, Frank tried to imagine himself feeding the baby, burping the baby, walking the baby, changing the baby. He tried to imagine Girl Scouts and Little League. Appalled though he was at the prospects, unnerved by his own inertia, rational as always in his own mind, there was still something about his wife he didn't dare confront – not, anyway, until she put her underclothes back on. Then he had to tell her what he thought. But after their discussion, Theo's nightmares returned. She woke screaming. He held her, wanting her more then than he ever had when she had wanted him. She fought him. She held her thighs together as tightly as if she were gripping something there, corncobs maybe.

"Theo," he pleaded.

"Screw your clients," she hissed.

At last he desisted. Three days later she miscarried anyway.

"It was all over then," Frank tells Billy. "Just when we had it so good."

Billy weeps for all of them.

If Frank ever suffered from guilt, he never admitted it; but Frank is not the most reliable of sources. He did quit social service soon after, right in the middle of the seventies. "I did my time," he said, "twice the average tenure in the field." And then he clipped his beard into a style and started wearing vests, and he learned disco, and he invested in coffee. In his new life, not surprisingly, seduction played a new role, more complex and therefore more enticing. He discovered that as soon as he made it with his dance partner, they lost contests they would have won before. Frank didn't think his other performance was to blame, only he didn't really know. He made it with six of them (two seduced him) before finally deciding it was bad for his form, at which point he switched over to his customers. Not so easy as their predecessors, and more expensive, these women were not without charm, and for a couple of years Frank felt quite satisfied with their rare scents and multicolored sheets, all of which smelled more or less the same by the time they were done. Then, when he turned thirty-seven, suddenly Frank lost interest. Still an attractive man — a little on the thin side but with good muscle tone and a peculiar blond intensity — he reapproached his wife who, time being what it is, endured his clumsy overture with passive acquiescence, and once again they started making love.

"NOT passionately," Frank tells Billy, "but regularly. It was all right. It was good. That's why I can't understand why all at once, all at once..."

Billy makes an effort, but can't restrain himself. He dries his tears coyly and smiles. He hums.

"Billy," Frank says sharply.

Grinning, Billy taps his feet to his tuneless ditty.

"Goddammit, Billy. Stop that."

Billy keeps on humming.

Frank says, "I think I'll call her."

Billy says, "N-n-no!"

THEO would have put it differently. "We were regular all right," she would have said, "as regular as feeding time at your local, two-bit zoo, with about as much enjoyment only not so often." The comparison isn't accidental: Theo thinks of that time in her life as a kind of hibernation. It was odd, but though she knew about Frank's lovers, she couldn't make herself care. She just felt numb all the time, numb and ugly. You may assume her apathy derived from her husband's infidelity, but it didn't. It came from another kind of loss. For so long Theo had spent so much of her time doing Frank's laundry and soft-boiling Frank's eggs ("Three minutes, I said.

Three minutes exactly. Didn't I buy you a timer?") that finally, with no children, something happened, and just as the soul quits the body when it dies, Theo's imagination quit her soul. Poor dear, matching socks was almost more than she could bear: red sock, red sock; blue sock, green sock, green, green, damn. They had a garden, but she didn't plant tulips and gardenias anymore; she planted turnips, radishes, and beets. Unused, their stereo grew dusty. As Carter changed to Reagan she sighed and said, "So let there be a war. Who can stop it?" How, Theo wondered when she managed to wonder anything, or rather why, oh why had she ever left her cornfields?

And no, we shouldn't find the question strange, for surely we have asked it of ourselves. Not about Nebraska, but that isn't the point. The point is that what happened to Theo happened to so many of us. Our lives were one way, then they were another – less rich, sadder, and with something gone out of them suddenly – maybe sex, maybe children, maybe something altogether different. It doesn't matter what it was. What matters is that we felt numb too, just like Theo. I don't know. If we believed in heaven we might start counting up what's left and marking it off in anticipation of something better, but heaven's hardly credible anymore. Theo doesn't believe in it, or didn't then. Then she didn't believe in anything until, all those years after they'd put him away, Billy was released from what Theo calls *the institution* and what Frank calls *the hospital* and showed up in their front yard one February morning, hunched over by the lemon tree in his shiny green rayon suit, white socks showing several inches at the ankle, and with the slightest, strangest half-grin on his downturned face.

So Theo gets another chance. The only question is: *Do we?*

II. BILLY

BILLY was a bad boy; now he's an enigma. What I have to say here may therefore be unpleasant, may seem, as well, ambiguous, even contradictory. Billy is Billy, and though I'd like to offer explanations, all I've got are facts, straightforward, hard, and simple, the kind we've got accustomed to relying on.

They're one year apart in their ages, the brothers. Frank's older. Frank's also, though smaller, more attractive. These things shouldn't matter and maybe they don't, but while Frank was getting straight A's all through junior high school, Billy was getting stoned. That's how he spent his early adolescence. The twelve years after that he spent – what, mad? Let's say disturbed. One night when he was tripping on acid, just barely thirteen, Billy came home and lit matches to his acne. This sounds like your typical drug horror story, but Frank doesn't think so. And Frank recalls the incident with particular vividness, maybe because it reminds him of how, years before and for several years on end, Billy entertained himself electrocuting fish.

"It's easy," he told the school counselor. "Just put in the extension cord and turn on the switch."

The counselor, a sincere if arrogant and flimsy man, recommended therapy. The boys' mother, who always wore white (white lawn dresses, white slacks, sheer white negligées) told the counselor to mind his own damned business, she'd raise her damned sons by herself.

"But Mrs. Stevens," said the counselor, "the boys' father. What about the father?"

"You leave him out of this," she said. "He's none of your business either."

"I'm trying to help."

"Go to hell," she said, walking out.

This was their first and last meeting in that small town in northern California, and the nature of small towns is that everybody knows what someone's mother says to the school counselor, the color and weight of her nightgown, how her younger son behaves. Billy never knew his father and he hated his mother and he didn't really feel very good about the fish.

So he dismembered cats instead. *Here kitty, kitty, kitty:* you could hear him at all hours of the night, *here kitty*. God punished him with acne in his seventh grade year.

"IT WAS awful," Frank told Theo years later. "First he acted weird but looked the same as anyone else. Then one morning he didn't. He looked awful."

Theo looked up what he had in a book on skin diseases and cried for three days after: her Frank's little brother.

BILLY didn't cry about it. As far as he was concerned, justice was justice. But he started buying dope from the junior high school drummer. At first he used to buy one marijuana cigarette at a time, then stay after school to practice his saxophone. These moments show a different Billy, talented, passionate, and with absolute love for his music. Listen just a moment now, yes: that high sweet note, that wild scale. But when he blew on his saxophone — it's hard to know quite how to put this — his ravaged face became further inflamed. And a person knows something like that, even if he never sees himself reflected in the sousaphones.

Billy knew. As a consequence, though in class the teacher often made him play a certain passage over and over in front of everyone until he got it right, it was only alone, among the scattered chairs and music stands, that Billy could really let forth and wail. Day after day he wailed, drawing ever nearer to God. Also as a consequence, for the longest time Billy associated being stoned with the curious odor of cork oil, wet reed, and spit, as well as with religious ecstasy.

Frank, who in those days avoided his brother, did not witness these scenes and so does not remember them. He does, however, remember Rodeo Parades. Straight down the Miracle Mile they would march, Billy two rows over, one row up. On those days, always, the sky turned a harsh, strident blue, with the sun pale white and blazing and the temperature hovering at one hundred. All the players sweated beneath their black wool turbans, but Billy more than the rest, his pocked and pustuled face alarmingly red. In particular, Frank remembers how his brother stumbled through steaming piles of horse dung, never stepping around them like the others, head bent down at an absurd angle, fingers flapping oddly on the keys.

"He'd make his connections at the end of the parade," Frank told Theo one time when they had just received news that earlier that afternoon Billy, once again, had slit his wrists, "and then take off to be by himself, maybe at the train station, maybe at the irrigation canal where it splits off from the river across from the park."

"You could have stopped him," Theo said.

"It wasn't the drugs. It was his queerness, his solitary nature."

"That's what I mean. You could have stopped him. Only, of course, you avoided him."

Theo was making soup. She got out the eggplant, the tomatoes, the onions and laid them on the yellow table in a wash of pale winter sunlight. She thought a minute before adding carrots and zucchini. "Are we out of turnips?" she said. "I think we're out of turnips. Also celery." She started peeling garlic.

"Once I went to see him," Frank said.

"Have a drink," Theo said. "I don't want to hear it again."

"His face..."

"...was all infected and he didn't make sense."

"He never made sense, not even as a little boy. Remember the fish? Only damn it, Theo, he's my brother, and I love him."

Theo handed Frank bourbon. "Now please shut up. You've never loved anyone in your life and you know it."

After Billy burned himself, Mrs. Stevens selected a state hospital several hundred miles away and committed him there one autumn afternoon when his face was still swaddled with gauze. The admitting psychiatrist recommended plastic surgery.

"Just lock him up," Mrs. Stevens said. "He's not safe anymore. I don't want him around."

They locked him up: one year, four years, six years, twelve. And all during this time, much of which Frank spent in social service, Frank expressed sympathy and his deepest concern but never did one thing to get him out or even get him placed somewhere better. In this way Billy missed out altogether on the seventies.

To THEO, as she sautéed firmer vegetables, Frank, sipping bourbon, complained, "It's her fault. He should have been in therapy. And now it's too late."

"Too late? Do you mean because of his visions?"

"If that's what you want to call them, my dear, but the clinical term is delusion. All that penance, that love, and God."

Theo cut into the eggplant and smiled. "So you blame her, do you? What did she ever do?"

"She was more psychotic than he came close to being. Long after her lovers fell asleep, she lay there waiting for him with her black police issue flashlight."

"So she beat him."

"No. She dragged him into the bathroom and shined that light in his eyes, looking for redness, dilation."

"And what did you do?"

"I listened to them yell. I offered him Murine."

None of this was news to Theo. She'd heard it all before, about the police issue flashlight, the penance. But for the longest time she hadn't understood. In the beginning, at the drop-in center, it had seemed very tragic to her – Billy's hypersensitivity, his mysterious pathology, and then what she thought of as the maiming. He must have thought so too, she thought: what else could explain his conversion? In this she was not wholly wrong. No, it wasn't this that Theo was confused about, it was the ambiguous offer of Murine. Theo married Frank believing his gesture to his brother had been another act of faith, not one of cowardice. By the time she figured out her mistake, Billy had been stuttering nonsense to his angels for so long no one even imagined he would ever talk straight again.

Well, we were like that in those days, every one of us, if not wise in our own right at babble then sympathetic to it, as Theo was. It didn't matter what you said. Anything was fine – until you brought in angels, and then you lost your audience just like that. Don't get me wrong. I'm not suggesting there's no truth in babble. Rather, quite the opposite. We were quick enough to back off, after all, when things started seeming clear. Now they don't anymore, so we feel safe.

As for Billy, it's not for me to say whether he was right or wrong in what he saw or heard, or how he answered back. His soul is his own and there's no peering into it. I can, however, tell you that after several years in the institution and at the same time he stopped eating meat, Billy's occasional violent outbursts ceased. From time to time he did still try to kill himself, but this, he said, was to hasten his ascension. And oh yes, he started humming all the time, softly to himself. Or sometimes he hummed to the other patients, who seemed to like it. They smiled and nodded, and they told Billy things. Head bowed – more now, people thought, from humility than shame – Billy hummed through the vilest confessions, and so it was that absolution was achieved on both sides. For myself, I've never had a vision, so I don't know what they're like. Billy won't talk about his either. All he'll do is hum, but you can tell from how he hums that it's something very beautiful.

III. THEO AND BILLY AND ME

THEO and Frank did not make love for the first six months after Billy came to live with them. No part of this arrangement was part of an arrangement, not the celibacy, and certainly not Billy. For though Theo had her principles, Theo was ambivalent. She felt sorry for Billy and had lost a certain faith in her husband over him, but she wanted a baby – a baby, not an infantile grown man. So when, as it happened occasionally through the years, Frank felt a little guilty, Theo resisted the slightest suggestion his brother come to stay.

"You're the one who doesn't like goons," she said.

"I didn't say that," Frank said. "I *said* there's no point in creating new goons."

"That's not what you said."

"What I said is irrelevant. He's my brother."

"But it's only your conscience that's worrying you now, and don't expect me to help you assuage it. I'd like to, Frank, but, Frank, I just can't."

Their discussions went no further, and neither did their actions. As I said before, Frank made no real effort to get Billy out. That came as a surprise to both of them.

IT WAS February, a bright, clear day, with premature lavender plum blossoms bruising the sky all down the block. The morning newspaper was late. Theo had already been out to look for it twice. The third time she went out, he was standing by the lemon tree, his green suit – made greener against the yellow fruit – shining in the sun. And it was quiet, like a dream. Theo, who had never met him but knew him at once, asked him in for coffee because she didn't know what else to do. Though his shoes were black, shiny, and hard, Billy followed noiselessly up the brick steps, across the front porch, along the tile entry.

Theo said, "Do you want cream?"

Billy didn't answer. Theo gave him cream. Then she called Frank from the bedroom.

"I told you not to call me here. I'm grinding French Roast. It's a delicate...what?" Frank said. "Oh God, then he's escaped. Call the hospital. Have you called the hospital?"

Theo called the hospital.

"Last name first," the hospital said. "Are you next of kin?"

"It doesn't matter what I am. He's here. He could be dangerous."

"Billy's harmless," said the hospital. "Believe me, he's perfectly safe."

"But he escaped."

"No, we released him. We're mainstreaming clients. It's part of our program."

"Don't you mean deinstitutionalization?"

"He'll receive guidance and welfare. For now, don't excite him. And don't worry if he talks to himself. They all do that. It's nothing."

Theo called Frank back.

"Well," he said, "we'll just have to be patient." He paused. "How does he look?"

"It's noticeable, but not abhorrent," Theo told him. "I think they must have done something."

"Good, then. Well, be patient. It will be all right."

Theo was patient. Billy wanted to play Scrabble, so they played Scrabble. But Billy wasn't much of an opponent. If he couldn't make the words *God*, *heaven*, *angel*, or *love*, he simply passed, showing his decision with a gesture of his hand. Except for his humming, his manners were impeccable, but as soon as he lost, he wanted to play again. Theo never had the heart to tell him that, technically speaking, *God*, as he used it, is a proper noun and therefore illegal. They played all afternoon.

That night, undressing for bed, Frank said, "You don't have

to carry things too far, you know. I've had experience in this, and Billy's got to learn.''

So NOW there were two pairs of socks to be laundered and matched, two sets of eggs to soft boil, and twice as many times to scrub out the bathtub, but it was different. Theo, especially attracted to what she thought of as mysterious and inscrutable in Billy, found everything about him intriguing. She even liked his humming, which got into her head like a chant or incantation and was a comfort in her barrenness.

One day they walked up into the hills. With Frank, long before when they had gone on walks, Theo had always been panting to keep up, throat burning, muscles aching, never seeing anything. But Billy walked slowly and as if he were discovering things for the first time, as indeed, it occurred to Theo, he was. Without discrimination or preference, he'd stop to marvel at anything, lichen and scrub grass as imbued for him with God's unspeakable grace as extravagant vistas of lakes or panoramic views of mountains. Theo herself, following his example, began to pay strict attention. When he knelt to part ferns, she didn't know if they'd find toadstools there or wild irises, and she didn't care. Small, spotted spiders were beautiful to her. The tiniest gray stones took her breath away. At last they came to a clearing high above the lake and sat down to rest. Below, the water was deep green in places, in others almost sapphire; the steep banks, a fine iron red. An early spring sun warmed their backs; an inconstant wind cooled where they'd sweated. As dragonflies coupled all around them, Billy hummed. Theo was remembering Nebraska.

HERE is my story: I was fifteen, born in that valley myself and raised there, a wanderer by nature, who liked to swim, who liked to walk. Thus, I knew that landscape, but no other, perfectly. So the first time I crossed the coast mountains to the sea, I was trying to remember names of trees: tan oak, madrona, sequoia. It was past dark when I arrived. Fog came in the night. The next morning I woke to a changed world.

Remember: *I was fifteen. And a virgin.*

That day I spent wandering through mist-shrouded, moss-hung cedars, grass wetting me up my thighs, and everything I saw seemed carved into a promise more mysterious, more tender, more sublime than I would once have imagined possible. Yet I remember very little from those hours. I don't remember being cold. I don't remember feeling lost, though I must have been at times. I do remember that at some point the fog lifted. Then the world was changed again, but was no less beautiful or new. As for the ocean, what I had come to find, sometimes I followed along above it, sometimes the path dropped down to the beach, sometimes it veered up again and in through the forest and occasional meadows.

In one of those meadows, ringed by azaleas, I came upon a rock as massive as those which formed the sea cliffs, but a quarter mile inland and discrete. Oddly shaped, it bulged out on one side, curved in on the other. My instinct was to climb. Near the base, grasses and shrubs tough enough to support my weight grew out of crevices, but about a third of the way up vegetation died off. This was on the east side. To my left I found black stone steps, some natural, some crudely chiseled out. The forest dropped away behind as I ascended them – one hundred feet below, two hundred feet below. By the time I reached the top, dusk had already begun to fall and an ocean bird kept calling, not one I had heard before but since, yes, often enough. I stood very still, listening, while the sun disappeared into the farthest blue-violet ridge of the horizon. Soon after, mist welled up again from every strand of grass below, from white flowering bushes, from the juts and hollows of that slice of rock I could scan straight down to the dissolving meadow and out to the sea.

There are, I suppose, many ways of describing what happened then: how I, like the meadow, dissolved, turned within to a great silence, believed myself to be connected by the mist to all it touched. The bird continued to call. I climbed a short way down the sheer west face of the rock to a ledge from which, as dusk obscured everything but the closest black-stemmed ferns and small white mushrooms, I believed I could take one more step with impunity. I believed it would support me, that fog. I believed I'd be absorbed by it, and it, somehow, by me.

But I stayed where I was and the moment passed.

What I'd say is that in all of our lives there is a time between youth and whatever comes next when everything seems not only possible, but necessary. You're balanced on a cusp then, as I was on that rock. Only in life you can't stand still. You step out blindly and your illusions dissipate.

After that first night on the rock, season after season, there came a gradual diminishment in my capacity for feeling as alive as I did then. I began by regretting the loss quite painfully, but as time passed I grew accustomed to the dimming in myself, which I attributed to growing older, to maturity when I was feeling especially self-satisfied. If I were less than I might have been, I was sterner, more resolute, and not at all vulnerable, I thought. The exchange didn't seem even, but it seemed fair. I conceived of it as progressive.

Then, more than ten years later, I found myself in the Massachusetts Berkshires, and it was spring. This time I wasn't alone; I wasn't a virgin. Midnight slipped right into a lush New England dawn, softer and sweeter than any I could remember, and so full of birds I almost didn't hear the one I'd heard the first time years before. A little like Theo and Billy, we walked out into that morning and traced a path among newly leafed-out trees to another meadow from which another mist rose and where cows still slept. We stopped and listened to their snuffling. He put his hand on my shoulder. I touched him too. And then I knew that on the other side of the clearing, just beyond the tree line, never mind the hundred miles to it, there was another ocean.

I am old enough now to be less interested in my first vision of my first sea than I am in the diminishment that followed, than I am in my reawakening. For between the one and the other there is a kind of counterpoint, infinitely rich and various, and studded here and there with so many unexpected possibilities. It may seem that something is missing, but something also is present – not wisdom, I wouldn't go so far as to say that, but a kind of context maybe, from which I draw patience, a sustaining curiosity, and this new faith in the eventual recovery of all that I have known and lost, and will know and lose again.

So no, I can't tell you what it was when Theo first looked about her and knew she had to have it all. I'm not familiar enough with the landscapes of Nebraska to second-guess the sunsets there; she might have taken a lover. Whatever it was, it was enough to send her spinning off across the country, wild with a passion for life which, as I've suggested, slowly died. But, as I've also suggested, Theo gets another chance: when Billy turned to her that afternoon above the lake, she opened up her blouse for him.

IV. THEO AND ME

THERE are just a few more things: that Billy made love as reverently as he parted ferns; that Frank found them finally underneath the lemon tree and claimed his wife in anger one last time; and that when he took his brother off with him, Theo said, "So you still think will prevails over faith? I can't under-

stand that anymore." Frank, as usual, had no idea what Theo
was talking about. Billy did but wasn't much interested: time
means little to him, and distance even less. Thus, he made no
real effort to resist his brother's imperative mood and was as
delighted with the Red Lion Motor Hotel as he was with the
stucco apartment across town Frank moved them to three days
later. Billy especially likes the style there – California fifties –
and the two leaning palm trees in the asphalt lot out front,
imported, Frank insists, from San Diego. Frank would insist
on something like that as he tends these days to deny all but
the most rational explanation of anything. Not to do so would
be to admit that once he had a wife, whom he loved in his own
way, and now, inevitably, he doesn't. So Frank is following
baseball; Frank is investing in real estate. As for Billy, Billy's
learned to cook and to refrain from feeling – what, remorse?
lust? self-satisfaction? – just now. Billy has, after all, a certain
kind of patience. And whether or not he knows that Theo is
pregnant again seems oddly beside the point. I might assume
he was aware of the moment of conception, just as a woman
sometimes is. I might assume the opposite. It should matter, I
guess, as it should matter how both Frank and Billy feel, what
they'll do about this woman they have held in common, lost
in common. But the true thing is I don't care. I don't really care
about any of them but Theo.

Or perhaps it doesn't matter either she's at last got what she
wants. Perhaps I've told this story with as little thought for its
consequences as Theo has given to what it will mean to bring
up a child, potentially a goon, by herself. But I don't think so.
I think I have told it not because I once stood above the Pacific
Ocean and believed as fog came in that it might hold me; but
because so many years later, when even words had changed,
I used them and it did. I think I have told it because Theo
seems so happy now, humming softly to herself, and insofar
as this is a story about anything, it is a story about that. Now

in her fourth month, past the dangerous first trimester, Theo knows that this time all will go well. She delights that her breasts have already grown heavier. She likes to stand naked in front of the mirror and admire the new slight distension of her belly. It's a most admirable belly – white and smooth and delicately rounded. Theo sleeps with her hand just there. Theo's sleeping now, and so we'll leave her.

BUT WHAT'S that Billy says to Frank? "I think I'll call her." Frank says nothing.

One Pair Red,
One Pair Blue

JENNY frequently feels herself sliding down. It's a case of keeping things wound so tight the least slippage sets her in a tailspin abrupt and alarming enough that if she didn't take drugs — alcohol, Valium, mostly — she'd never get them wound again, and while Jenny doesn't care about herself much anymore, she cares about her son, who would suffer. Yet to see her a person would never expect it, the dark erratic side, the wild emotional swings. Jenny, not particularly attractive, blends in. If you should see her at the health clinic, for example, or unloading her groceries at the check-out stand, or pumping discount gas, or paying bills, she'd look like all the other working mothers, wearing sandals and a flared skirt that falls just below her knees, and probably an ironed cotton blouse. Her few attempts at fixing herself up seem designed more to deflect attention than attract it. This is California, so the glasses she's worn all her life have a light gray tint. Once a day she glosses her lips and applies just a touch of mascara. And Prue thinks she has worked on her tan, which is darker than she remembers Jenny's natural complexion and a little more deliberately even. That's about it. Jenny comes and goes from her small, neat house with an air of determination and purpose. Once inside, she slips off her sandals and draws the curtains just enough to let light but not direct sun in. She gets a beer and settles in a frayed easy chair to wait for David to come home from school. Sometimes, to arrest her crazy plummet, she gets another beer, and sometimes that helps. As long as she doesn't think, she's all right, but David's on split session, second shift, and Jenny's off at noon.

Prudence is smaller than Jenny, shorter, less amply curved, but still she stands out more in a crowd: is this calculated? Certainly, Prue dresses to call attention, mostly in outrageous shades of red — red socks, a red sweater, red tennis shoes. Otherwise, like Jenny, she does not appear in any way to be remarkable. Prue's ex-husband once observed to her that she had suffered more than any woman he'd ever known over not being beautiful; he meant, of course, being bland. Her features are pleasant, but ill-defined. Her exactly average weight is evenly distributed over an exactly average frame. She wears her straight brown hair clipped blunt at shoulder length. The single possible exception to Prue's outward lack of distinction is her voice. Not that she sings (though she'd like to, she's tone deaf) but that when she speaks there's a certain earnest quality in how she phrases things and self-consciously modulates them — at times just short of shrill. Prue herself prefers to think she sounds sincere.

Jenny's and Prudence's friendship goes back a long way, long before Davie, long even before Marco, to the cat they dissected one day in high school that touched, quite unexpectedly, the same nerve in both of them which still, more than ten years later, strikes a sympathetic resonance whenever they meet, not so often since they've gone their different ways. Prue doesn't know if it's the divergence or the ways themselves that keeps bringing her back in this nervous circle. All she knows is that twice before she's tried to tell the story, and as this makes the third, she is uneasily aware of how much she presumes each time she changes fact to narrative. Yet Prue has her own ideas of obligation and salvation, and if she is the only one who needs to tell what happened, who indeed conceives of this particular configuration of events as a story at all, she can only protest: how could she not? While Jenny, in her easy chair, doesn't think in terms of stories, for how could she?

Thus, what Prue wants more than anything is to get the beastly facts down without hurting anyone, and as precisely as memory will allow. In her mind, they look somehow like fate, or even destiny, she thinks, as if Jenny's life was determined without her. Prue shrugs. Poor dear. She'd like to offer her friend something extravagant and meaningful – a cold imported beer, a handshake instead of a kiss. But Jenny drinks Coors. Prue flinches at the word, which she means nonetheless in its truest, most difficult, and dispassionate sense: she *loves* Jenny. As for Jenny, it's hard to say exactly how she feels about Prue, assuming she feels anything at all. For Jenny's gone to sleep.

I. THE FIRST TIME

PRUE played glockenspiel in the high school marching band. Jenny twirled the baton. For two years they took pains whenever they had to – lining up at half time, selling brownies at the annual bake sale – to be polite to each other, but reserved. Theirs was not so much a distance of personality as of class. Jenny didn't even go to school in town until her freshman year, not even junior high. There was still that one-room schoolhouse near her family's dirt-poor ranch. Whereas Prudence had her social standing, her pretensions. During home canning season Jenny's fingers were stained; in the spring she smelled of manure. Already she was broad-hipped and full-chested, and the homemade clothes she wore – coordinated, unlike Prue's store-bought, more for function than for fashion – served largely to accentuate her prematurely matron-like presence. The two girls had different lunch periods, which at the time they thought nothing about.

But moments exist in all of our lives which, however unre-markable as they occur, in retrospect seem pivotal, as if, if that one thing had never happened, everything else would be different. There are people who would argue that's true of every moment, each one leading irretrievably to the next, but Prudence doesn't think so. She doesn't, for instance, place much importance on the particular sequence of circumstance and chance that ended with both her and Jenny in the same sopho-more biology class. She doesn't feel strongly that the teacher, a gray-haired religious zealot, assigned lab partners by a quirky manipulation of sex, seating chart, and whim. Both sets of events seem meaningless and arbitrary to her. But that Jenny wanted to stay after school and work on her technique the same October afternoon Prue's orthodontist changed her regu-lar appointment, and that it was the first stormy day of the year with a high wind and massive black-centered clouds and the same day Jenny's brother got his draft call, all seem to Pru-dence, looking back, significant in the extreme, with such far-reaching implications.

Jenny didn't want to talk about her brother then. She didn't want to talk at all. What she wanted was that Prue should hold the animal in just a particular way so she might make the first incision clean. They worked in silence on opposite sides of the long black table. Prudence ran her tongue along her braces. Jenny paused occasionally to bite at formaldehyde-toughened cuticles. There was that smell, acrid, but made poignant with the coming on of autumn's sweet, bleak dusk, and there was the sound of their instruments on the hard, rubberized sur-face. Distracted, Prue kept trying to remember Jenny's brother, Gary she thought his name was, a little on the chunky side, crew cut, and with a pale grainy-textured complexion prone to blushing at such times as when the girls were all measured for new band uniforms. Hadn't he played last trumpet? She wiped her hands, took her turn clipping sinews from feline musculature, and wondered what it would be like for him in Vietnam. Across from her, Jenny was poking intently at the place between the heart and the lungs. Prudence thought suddenly of Gary's heart, similarly vulnerable. Jenny glanced up and met her eye. That was all but more than enough, for in that one instant it was as if they'd shared a single thought, and finding it unthinkable, dismissed it both together. At home that night Prue listened, really listened, to the network war reports.

Still, it was months before they acknowledged their complicity, months during which their friendship developed in the most banal and superficial of ways. Jenny showed Prudence how to milk her 4-H goat and trip the baton through her fingers. She shared her best diagrams and lab notes, and at Christmastime gave Prudence hot homemade pepper jelly, red with flecks of green suspended in it. Prudence, who wanted a more – what, intimate? – friendship but didn't know how, found herself combing her closet, trying to decide which of last year's clothes she might give Jenny. She tactfully broached the subject of makeup. She ran down the current top-ten tunes. As it happened, Jenny took the clothes but didn't wear them, and Prudence got an eye infection from mascara. The one remained serious and imperturbable, while the other couldn't wait for something terrible and real to happen.

Gary came home on leave from Fort Ord looking more red-faced than ever and anxious to be off to Vietnam. Prudence tried praying for him. Jenny rode her horse into the hills and, in the months that followed, took to wearing beads and armbands and to organizing things – boycotts, moratoriums, like that. The scale was small but not to Prudence, who watched her friend's political ascension with something close to reverence, something close to grief. Jenny worked these difficult things out so quickly, so decisively, as if the terrible and real held neither dread nor fascination for her, but simply were, palpable realities to be reckoned with and, if possible, defused. But Prue, for all her prayers and odd susceptibility to faith and despite her keen desire for transcendence, was incapable of Jenny's unselfconscious commitments, bordering, it often seemed to Prue, on the euphoric. Only when Jenny insisted did she cut herself an armband from her eighth-grade glee club skirt and then, because of her parents, kept it hidden at school among the dirty gym socks in her locker. Every morning when she put it on and every afternoon when she took it off, Prue felt meek and small and, so often these days, like crying. For Christmas she and Jenny sent cookies to Gary, who wrote they'd arrived broken and stale. The girls sent brownies wrapped in foil. Gary wrote where was the dope? Prudence thought he meant it to be funny, but Jenny smiled like she knew something and wasn't talking. Then Jenny started dating the black class president. Jenny got birth control pills. Prue touched herself at night to find out what she might be missing but felt nothing and wept instead. No one's blouses matched their skirts anymore: who wore skirts?

This went on for another year until, by the end of high school, Prue was both sorry and relieved Jenny's antiwar activities had lost her the scholarship she might have once received, while she, whose parents were paying, would be going away in the fall. But once again she had misjudged their loss, and so they tried to compensate through correspondence, exchanging recipes by mail, confessing sexual encounters. Time passed. They wrote less often and hence more passionately. Both wanted to believe the perfect baring of their souls would make them close again; both knew in their hearts that was a lie. Thus, by the time Jenny finished at the local junior college with enough money saved to go where Prudence went, Prue had a new life she wasn't so anxious to share. There were things about Jenny she tried to remember – how proud she'd been to listen to her speak against the war, the flowers she'd twisted around her silver baton. Instead, she felt ashamed of the baton itself. She couldn't make herself forget that even in peace marches Jenny's jeans hadn't been faded Levis but some other kind with a dark thread running through them, shiny and stretchy and too tight around the hips.

Prudence needn't have worried, for Jenny, who came quietly on the bus and settled down to her studies as assiduously as she had once attacked her politics, had changed in those two years during which the war still didn't end and Gary reenlisted. She didn't want to meet Prue's current lover. She wasn't interested in drug connections. Prue wanted to conceive of her friend's restraint as a self-effacing deference, but it was hard. Jenny was already accumulating honors more rapidly and impressively than Prudence ever would. If Prue were praised for a paper, Jenny was asked to present one. Prue took second place in a local short story contest, but Jenny was asked to study foxes for the summer on an island off the coast of Santa Barbara. So Jenny had it all again, even without trying, and Prue couldn't help but resent it. When they passed each other on the college paths now, their smiles were uncharacteristically forced, and they stopped less frequently to chat. Only if they couldn't avoid it would they sit together in the cafeteria.

Still, it was Prudence Jenny asked for dinner that night early on in their final term, and still Prudence accepted. Jenny was living by the Boardwalk so Prue took the cliff road, putting off by walking what she felt sure would be an awkward evening. It was a long, tender dusk, full of gulls and the first rollercoaster screams of the season and so many hardy surfers. A pale crescent moon shaped like a woman's earring hung low out over the water. Prue wanted very much to remain as night deepened. She thought there might be iridescent tides. But

Prue, who still maintained her loyalties, bought bourbon instead and hurried on to find Jenny sautéeing vegetables and listening to jazz on a cheap radio. The bourbon was a good idea. Eagerly they drank it straight and warm from the bottle and continued to drink it throughout dinner.

Later they sat on a torn floral couch, still keeping at the bottle. Jenny talked about her foxes for awhile, her voice low and soft as if she loved them very much. Prue talked about a paper she was writing on the Brontës. They seemed to be doing so well with their pretense, but suddenly Jenny was crying. Prue, alarmed, thought at once of Gary; but when she tried to ask, her voice sounded odd and hollow and she stopped. In the same instant Jenny did too, as abruptly as she'd started. Behind them in the darkened window a bullet hole refracted and distorted the yellow streetlamp outside, the lights of the Chinese grocery across the street. Prudence thought she could look at the world that way forever. So calm it was more like a dream than anything as final as it turned out to be. Jenny announced she was saying good-bye, dropping out, changing courses once again. Nine half-completed credits short of graduation, Jenny was leaving school.

THIS, then, was the first time Prue tried to tell the story. It was odd, but she didn't think about why she wanted to tell it. That was instinct. What she thought about was how difficult it was and in so many ways beyond her, for when she looked at the facts they seemed, not extraordinary as she knew they were, but common and pedestrian: *Dirt-poor valley rancher's daughter throws promising future away.* Prudence wanted to transform those facts, she wanted to get close to their essence, and she wanted herself out of it. This was Jenny's story, she insisted to herself, unable to forget how Jenny had looked. *Thin,* she realized in retrospect: Jenny had been thin. And she couldn't remember ever having seen her cry before either. There was

something in those tears, Prudence thought, signifying —
what? That's what she wanted to tell.

So she thought about it for a long time before finally selecting a moment that never took place. In it she and Jenny were
sixteen and had ridden Jenny's father's horses out through
hills which, though she'd lived among them all her life, Prue
had never seen like that before. All morning they had followed
a cottonwood-studded creek bed, yellow with autumn, and
Prue had been deeply impressed by Jenny's manner with the
animals, how competent she was, and calm, how cleanly she
rode. Now they were seated on a flat red rock above a many-
fingered lake eating sandwiches of thick cheese and garden
tomatoes, sharpened with mustard. The two horses snuffled
behind them. Above, voluminous clouds massed and broke
apart, massed and broke apart. A little shyly, a little coyly, the
girls eyed each other, full of longing for all they believed they
would soon be discovering together.

Even now Prue is drawn to this moment, for which when
she wrote it she found herself yearning with an almost inconsolable sense of regret that it didn't happen, that she wasn't
there. What attracts her is not its pastoral quality, though there
is that, not even all they might have said to each other within
it, but just this: her sudden, unexpected insight that Jenny was
not what she seemed, that inside the broad-hipped, baton-
twirling 4-H'er there was a sensibility that saw the world in a
colder, clearer light than Prue had yet imagined, a sensibility
that placed Jenny in a context richer and more full of ambiguity
than Prue could ever hope to fathom.

After awhile a hawk swooped down low above some split-
trunked Digger pines, and wind rose up off the lake. The two
girls brushed hair back from their faces, glanced once more at
each other, then away, down, perhaps, at their feet. Each for
her own reasons wanted to touch the other, but neither did.
And yes, that was all Prudence managed the first time, in part

because she was young and inept at invention, in part because she believed then that everything, all feeling and knowledge, could be contained in a single inarticulate moment, filled only with instinct. Her instinct was that she *knew,* she knew something about Jenny. But as she couldn't say what, finally she could do no better than to defer to the image she herself had created and which still comes to her sometimes before sleep of her and Jenny as young girls, tired from their horseback ride and resting after lunch on a flat, expansive rock above a windswept lake, both staring intently down at their tennis shoes: one pair red, one pair blue.

II. THE SECOND TIME

MARCO is, well Marco was, a biker who bought and sold used cars through the paper and invested in beer parlors. Before that he worked almost nine months at a corner import market where every morning it was his responsibility to put out fresh vegetables and straighten the shelves – green chilies in the Mexican aisle, hot sesame oil in the Chinese. In spite of himself Marco found he enjoyed the long hours, the sweet and pungent smells and colors of the vegetables and labels, as well as the young girls who came in with their babies, buying whatever was cheap. Marco used to watch the babies and chew at the inside of his lip, sometimes biting off little chunks of skin. That was when he was with his first wife, the one who had tricked him into marriage when she knew all along she could never have a baby because of a botched abortion when she was fifteen. When Marco found out, it was bad.

Prue isn't looking for reasons, but Marco's grandmother, who raised him, lived half her life in Mexico and never learned English. Thus, between her and Marco there was a problematic world of difference. It was especially hard for Marco because he didn't much like the way he turned out and would gladly have pleased her if he only knew how. Marco didn't look the part (his jeans rode low beneath his paunch, his torn T-shirts hiked above) but Marco was a haunted man – haunted by his father, who had left him to go back to his own country; haunted by his mother, who had done her best to give him that advantage she sacrificed so much for, including, finally, him; haunted by his grandmother, who patted fresh tortillas out by hand, sang lullabies in Spanish, and survived harder times than either of Marco's parents ever came close to; haunted, finally, by his son, whom he loved fiercely, though that came later. In another culture, perhaps, in another time, Marco might have been successful, respected, a family businessman in the most honorable tradition. But Marco was born in L.A. in the forties and raised there, and he got out the only way he could. Prudence, who has gotten ahead of herself, is convinced that Jenny alone understood all this in the haunted man she married one careless day in Reno when she was eight months pregnant and Marco just jackpotted two dollar slots.

That was how it was with Jenny three years after she left school. The first two years Prue heard nothing, until gradually she stopped thinking about it so much. Then sometime during the third year she ran into Gary, one-armed since his final tour, at a seedy North Beach bar where she sometimes went to get material for poems, as after college Prue became a poet. They had drinks while Gary told her that even Jenny's family hadn't heard from her for months and that the first they even knew was when Jenny's old landlord came to them for back rent. That was when he was laid up too. But as soon as he could he went down to check it out. Jenny just left everything behind, not even taking the quilt she had made, not even cleaning up after her dinner with Prue. Gary ordered another double. Prudence remembered to write down Jenny's address before agreeing, well all right, to join him.

Still it was three months before Prue got as far east as Fresno and even then she was only passing through on her way to a poetry workshop in the Sierras, but she'd gotten a rather earlier than necessary start and so decided, more on impulse than anything else, to drop by. What she found was a concrete two-tiered apartment complex, long and painted pale green. White lines in the asphalt lot marked places for cars, one for each door. At the second level, twenty tiny cement decks, cluttered with hibachi barbecues and motorcycles, stuck out from paned glass doors. Immediately below, the first floor apartments had small mangy plots of grass, similarly littered. The number Prue had began with a two. She climbed the stained concrete steps trying not to wonder why she'd come.

And then Jenny, largely pregnant, answered the door in striped house slippers and an orange Hawaiian print muu-muu. It was not, in the end, a long story. Three years before, she had taken a dawn bus out of town and by evening had found work in a cannery. That was all right, she told Prudence. By midnight the cannery cooled down, and they were always working something sweet and pretty – peaches, tomatoes, small sleek-skinned plums. When the season ended she started serving beer in one of Marco's doomed investments. She didn't take drugs and she wasn't promiscuous, but she liked the sexuality of it, the pink hot pants, the black slit skirts. The first year she lived in a motel apartment at the Paradise Villa where the cracked swimming pool, never filled, collected leaves and soda cans and the wrappers of every brand of cigarette. After that she lived with Marco, not where Prudence found her but someplace like it. The first manager was prejudiced against bikers, but this one rode along so things were better. Things were fine, Jenny said. She patted her large belly. How had it gone with Prudence?

They passed the morning that way, talking and drinking iced coffee on the filthy green shag carpet. An old nine-inch fan in the window blew the hot August air of the valley desul-

torily around. Children played loudly in the parking lot below.
Prue had gotten, since she'd last seen Jenny, more adept at
appearances, so it sounded good enough, what she said, but
it wasn't. Of the two of them Jenny was by far the more
convincing. And without any lover at all that year and, if she
were honest, sick to death of poetry, Prue was anxious enough
to believe her friend had pulled it off again. Maybe happiness
wasn't the right word for the way Jenny seemed, but a certain
satisfaction, yes, verging on contentment. There were maga-
zines but no books in the apartment.

By the time Marco joined them later they had switched to
beer and moved out onto the deck. With three of them there it
was crowded. They kept bumping knees and awkwardly re-
adjusting their aluminum patio chairs, often drinking acciden-
tally from someone else's can. To compensate they laughed a
great deal and opened new cans until everyone was drunk.
Marco's stomach, Prue noticed, was very flat, very firm; his
chest was broad, and he'd rolled a pack of cigarettes into the
sleeve of his T-shirt. Tattoos ran all the way down his arm.
Liquor made him talk with maybe some small remaining trace
of an accent, and to Prue his voice sounded resonant and
moving. All night as he held forth on why we should have
nuked Vietnam and the way his woman humped like a whore,
she just kept feeling trite and self-consciously aware that her
own skirt was too long, her hair too severe, her bracelet, a gift
from an ex-lover who made jewelry, too heavy and too silver,
the soles of her shoes too conspicuously wood.

PRUE didn't go to the poetry workshop in the Sierras. She
went home and sold her jewelry instead, and told everyone
she knew she was through with writing anything at all. Of
course she wasn't, but she had no way of knowing then the
sheer accumulation of experience in her own life had dulled
her appetite for invention. Prue was tired. She was particu-

larly tired of crafting elegant, rarefied poems no one read or
cared much about. She didn't care herself, believing as she
now did that Jenny had achieved through simple daring the
kind of satisfaction in her life all Prue's deliberations had not
achieved for her. Perhaps for the first time, Prue thought of it
as fate and went out and got herself a new job as a typist.

Only if Jenny was Jenny, Prudence was Prue. Altogether it
took less than three months typing memos, a new vasec-
tomized lover, and Jenny's Reno postcard announcing she had
married and delivered in the same week, to set Prue spinning
back to her old habits. What she said now was she'd been
waiting for a sign.

This time when she tried to tell the story Prue was not
romantic, but analytical. As she explained to her lover, the
way events happened in their exact order and timing could
mean only one thing, and her task, in telling it over, was to
divine that meaning out of the many conflicting signals life
itself put in the way. This, Prue said, depended not so much
on reconstruction as on interpretation: *Ah that*, she added
strangely, *that's the gift*. The lover, impressed, proposed. Prudence decided that in Jenny's case Jenny wanted something
out of life – differentiation from her family, a good job, professional achievement – but when she saw the sham in her ambi-
tion, took something else instead, closer to the heart of human
struggle, more difficult, and therefore, Prue dislikes the term
but finds it apt, realer. Yes, Jenny was real. At first Prue thought
of Marco as the signifier, being the most unlikely choice and
thus the most divine. Later, when Jenny called long-distance
to say Marco was drinking too much, Marco had lovers, Marco
was out of work and running out of money, Prue was anxious
to admit she had been wrong. Davie was the sign. For Jenny,
who had dared so much in such baffling ways, had also dared
to have a son. Prudence thought about that for awhile before
reluctantly deciding to go ahead and marry her infertile lover.

Davie had two blue eyes at birth but one of them turned brown. Jenny said that was the start of it — that, and his persistent colic. She shrugged. Marco believed that boys, from the earliest time in the cradle, should demonstrate machismo. Prue, who had driven half the night to come and get her, said not to talk about it now. Jenny tried to smile but her lip was swelling where it had been split. She wouldn't see a doctor until they got to San Francisco.

In the three weeks she and Davie stayed with Prue in Prue's husband's Pacific Heights apartment, Jenny filed for divorce and Prudence grew as fond of the clumsy toddler as if he were her own. Davie was a large child, betrayed by his own body. His limbs, too heavy for his muscles, resisted his will. To compensate, he made up such amusing tales — where the ball went, what tripped him — that Prue, enamored anyway of his different-colored eyes, would gladly have put them both up indefinitely. But Jenny was busy with lawyers and had her principles in any case: nothing could dissuade her from returning. A boy, she explained late at night over brandy and over and over to Prudence, should know his father. His father, Prue replied, doesn't even *like* him. Not *him*, *me*, Jenny explained. Besides, Marco loved him and that was different.

Jenny was right. Marco did love Davie, enough to pick him up one day at the appointed time and not to bring him back for eighteen months. When he did, Davie took one look at his mother and started screaming. *You're dead*, he seemed to be saying, *you're dead, you're dead, you're dead!* Marco shrugged. What else was there to tell him? Jenny was trying not to, but Jenny was crying. Marco had a new wife now, and anyway a boy should know his mother.

ALL THIS last Prue never even tried to tell, though sometimes she thought she might have wanted to if there were any way to do it without making things worse. But she saw Jenny off and on through those long months and nothing in her own life helped her make sense of what she saw. Jenny had started drinking. Jenny had gotten fat. Jenny hid her hair under kerchiefs and her pasty-colored skin was broken out. Prue took another gin and tonic herself and did not think about her own bad marriage. What she thought was how she had come to the end of her stories. She had been wrong. There was nothing left to tell.

III. THIS LAST TIME

PRUDENCE was wrong again, but she wouldn't know that for another five years, during which she got divorced and moved back home, while Jenny got a job, bought a house, and settled down to try and salvage what she could of her life and son. That last part wasn't easy, but Jenny was patient and in time Davie got over the feeling he was living with a ghost. Slowly, his nightmares became less persistent, less violent, less horrifying to his mother. Not with that wife but with the next Marco fathered a daughter. Davie came to love her absolutely and planned to marry her when he grew up.

In this way, Prue arrives at the present, or nearly so. Almost she has come full circle, back around to the desire that she might efface herself. But Prue was concerned with personalities then, as if she could fathom them. Now she knows she can't, she'll render any surface. For Prue's not making things up anymore and instead sees the facts as opaque. How unnerving she finds it, but necessary. Prue drinks brandy now, nipping at the bottle. She nips. She takes her head between her hands. Nevertheless, she persists.

THAT Christmas, for the first time in years, a group of old high school classmates who had banded together against the war and then gone off to school and separate lives were visiting their parents. This would have meant little to Prudence except it was Jenny who called to invite her to their party. Prue tried to make herself look good, and went.

From the start she felt it was a mistake. The house was close and the wine pretentious. One woman, who had been very fat, was now thin; a thin one was fat. There were lawyers and graduate students, a city planner, a psychologist. Prue remembered all their names and enough about their pasts to know she could know nothing about them anymore, nor would she care to. She drank her wine quickly and then poured herself another glass. Jenny didn't arrive for what seemed a long time.

Prue doesn't know. Perhaps because she was depressed about her own life to begin with, or perhaps because she now felt guilty about her past preoccupations and descriptions of her friend, but when Jenny did arrive, neatly dressed and with an air of well being about her, despite Prue's impulse to call out to her, embrace her, engage her in conversation, she retired instead to a corner of the room where she remained for the rest of the afternoon. Someone talked to her about geology. She thought perhaps she had slept with him once. Someone else told her about France. As no one asked about her, she told nothing. She was obsessed with the sound of Jenny's voice without being able to separate the words. That was another conversation. She had more wine and wanted to go.

Then the first person left. And then three more all at once. The room seemed to clear. Jenny, alone now, crossed over to Prue, offering a polite embrace which Prue did not resist, though afterwards she smiled awkwardly and couldn't think of what to say. They exchanged pleasantries. Jenny liked her job, Davie was a good boy, she'd been sorry to learn Prue had divorced. Prue was glad to hear it. No, that was all over now. Jenny gave her a sympathetic look, not quite a smile. She knew about that too, she said. But it was time to go. She embraced Prue again and said how nice it was to see her. Then, almost as an afterthought, in parting, she added: *Marco shot himself last fall, and he shot his wife and his baby daughter and his roommate and his roommate's girlfriend.*

WELL, and that's what, in the end, everything reduced to, for all these many words just these few: *Marco shot himself last fall, and he shot his wife and his baby daughter and his roommate and his roommate's girlfriend:* the end of the story, the beginning of the story, the whole story in every manifestation it's ever assumed. Prue wishes it could have ended differently but thinks it will still be all right. If nothing else she's glad it's finally finished. For when she thinks of Jenny now, she thinks of nothing but how she turned and said what she said. She might have been holding a wineglass, Prue can't remember. If she was, she must have put it down. Her eyes were clear and her hair neatly styled. She said what she said. And she left.

But really Prue doesn't think much about Jenny anymore. Not that she doesn't still love her but that she has her own life to get on with. There's that. She's going back to school, moving east. And there's Davie. Sometimes Prue thinks about Davie, who is eight now. Still a big boy, the biggest in his class this year, he's learned to turn his size and his startling, mismatched eyes to his advantage. For the most part he's well mannered about it, helping the teacher move desks around, carrying the heaviest stack of library books, but every once in awhile he rears his bulk back in such a way that whatever the other child was going to say somehow never gets said. To look into his blue eye, his brown eye at such moments is to look into the eyes of someone more than twice his age and inconsolably embittered. His method of intimidation, largely unconscious, is not purely physical. There's another element to it which, once or twice, has even unnerved Jenny. On those nights she finds herself staring back at her son with something very close to animal fear. So for the thousandth time she reads to him from *The Little Prince* until he falls asleep with his head in her lap. And then she takes him off to bed and pours herself a whiskey, for it's late enough for that, and settles down in her frayed easy chair, not to read, not to watch TV, not to think or dream or wish it were all different, but just to sit there in her easy chair and drink, and then to sleep.

Bear and Other Pale Giants

I.

IN THAT family there were two weddings in five years. I say *that* when of course I mean my family, only Aunt Florence's side. She was the first to be wedded, and then her daughter Abbie, short for Abigail Rose, after my mother, Rose. For Aunt Flo, it was her second legal union and though later it appeared to be a marriage of convenience, at the time everyone said it was a whirlwind romance. They said it with an air of self-congratulation, as if they somehow had a hand in it: poor Flo! Though she was married two times, she adhered to the old school, loving only one man in her life, and him not either time her husband. My mother and her mother called this man to whom Aunt Florence remained faithful in her heart my Aunt Flo's "one true love"; but anyway, he didn't make it through the Second World War.

"Snuffed out in the promise of his manhood," said my father when he drank and reminisced.

"New Guinea," said Grandmother Georgia. "Where's that?"

The next-of-kin sent Florence not his medals, but the buttons off his uniform, which Flo polished and kept in a velvet-lined pouch, and a photo, dimly lit, of the deceased beside a man-sized flower. Her first husband was a reaction. He had asthma and a tendency toward drink. Her second was the one we mistakenly believed had swept her off her feet. I was twelve when they married in the parlor of the main house one brilliant autumn afternoon during the Cuban missile crisis.

"If they start anything while we're away," my mother said to my father in the car on the way to the wedding, "I swear I will never forgive her."

"Now calm down," he told her. "Relax. I mean it. A crisis is not a war."

We arrived in the late morning and entered at the kitchen door, the one the family always used, more out of habit than intimacy. At least two times a year we went to see Aunt Florence, often after Christmas, and then in the summer for the Fourth of July. We liked to think we bore up well under the stress of this familial duty, performing it punctually and with good humor, though in truth it was never easy for us. At home, as the time of each visit approached, Mother's anxiety could be felt as a palpable dread. I have never understood what exactly disturbed her—regret perhaps, or guilt, maybe envy—but I don't think she did either, because she used to complain most bitterly about Florence's roses. Flo benefited, of course, from the graces of nature, helped along as she was by the rich coastal soil and damp climate; but she had a talent for it too, and did grow extravagant gardens, which in comparison to the meager flower beds my mother tried to grow in the red, clayey soil and heat of the interior where we lived, seemed a personal affront that increased my mother's standard sense of deprivation to one of almost tangible loss. Summer was hardest, and the rare spring, when even the crude ice plant on the dunes turned pink and purple; but Flo's winter cacti bloomed with pernicious regularity too, and the leaves of her poinsettias were always splendid.

Fortunately, as I said, my aunt was married in the autumn.

So the flowers in her house were not her own, but from the florist's; and if the frail underscent of last season's roses still pervaded in corners and cupboards, it was difficult to distinguish among the many stronger, celebratory odors: coffee, sweet cream, raspberry champagne punch. My mother helped herself to coffee from an urn. My father asked for, and got, a double martini: "On the rocks, just a *psst* of vermouth."

The way it is with families, when a member of one marries, everyone comes to approve or disapprove, depending on the circumstances. So it was at Aunt Florence's wedding. Grandmother Georgia presided. We came from the valley. And Aunt Betty Sue, related by marriage to my dead Uncle Kurt, drove around from the other side of the bay. With my cousin Abigail, that was all of us, and a few family friends: Flo's hairdresser, the antique dealer, one or two who remembered my Grandfather Bear. Father, martini in hand, stood out on the lawn as the cars approached, as if by overseeing their arrival he might intercept the verdict before it was quite in. Compelled by the same impulse, he also read the paper every morning and stocked our cellar with fresh water and canned beans. My father was a man who tried to count on everything; however, in this instance he did not count on Betty Sue.

Betty drove too fast around the curved dirt drive, swerving too close and ripping the branches of the willow. The family, already assembled, took her arrival as a cue. Father came in from outside. Mother stopped deviling eggs. Georgia stood from where she'd been arranged, half-dwarfed, in Bear's enormous wingbacked chair. Florence positioned herself by the door to greet her guest properly. And though we assumed our preparations for resistance were discreet, in fact the room was rigid with a single shared thought: by any decent standards, and most especially ours, black becomes a widow until she is a bride.

But Betty didn't seem to notice, or if she noticed, to be

bothered much by our censure, appearing on the contrary to bear the shame of her preference for life over grief with enthusiasm. Dressed in a bright yellow sheath with blue trim, she had rouged her cheeks and lips and, I think, touched up her gray. There was something unseemly about her as she straightened her dress about her hips and half strutted on heels an inch or two too high. So it was coolly and with a stern, humorless thrust of the chin that Florence turned her own lightly powdered cheek front and up to Betty for the obligatory peck. We were all watching as they embraced stiffly, then broke apart. Betty smiled; Florence nodded, but without expression. Betty gave a small cry and flung her arms once again around the other's shoulders. In our strained silence, her voice as she exclaimed, "I am so happy for you!" was shrill and too loud. Everybody heard.

Thus the verdict came not, as we expected it, from consensus on the quality or the future of the match, but rather from our instinct for consolidation. Betty's approval was something to be outdone, a presumption we took as a challenge to exclude her further with our own worthier blessing. My allegiance, of course, was correct. On the one side, my mother's blood-related sister wore scrupulous off-white and a corsage of yellow flowers – dahlias, perhaps, very matronly. Halfway up her thigh, the linen of her skirt bulged with the suspicion of what I knew was sure to be there. Her unfrivolous hands seemed resplendent in their nakedness, awaiting the beatified ring. Whereas Betty Sue, a marital relation only, on three fingers wore rhinestones that blazed with each overly dramatic inclination of her wrist. Through the open toes of her patent leather heels, I could see the red polish on her nails. Her cigarettes were long and thin and stained at the butts from her lipstick. Thus, it was only natural that my affection should go to my real aunt, whose dignity and radiance made Betty seem cheap. The one embodied perfect love, the other desecration, and the dominance of the former was so absolute in my imagination that, beside it, even the frightful possibility of war that weekend was mercifully diminished. Everything but the wedding was a dream – distant, substanceless, benign.

All day only one incident broke that spell, a single, unexpected splitting off of events that remains, peculiarly, more vivid in my memory than the rest together. The adults were mingling as they waited for the minister, and I had settled in a corner, part from shyness, part to indulge more freely in my charged emotions. But before I could achieve my imagined union with the bride, Betty found me and engulfed me in a hug. Cut off from the others by the confusing tangle of her arms and breasts, I was unable to reorient myself quickly enough to prevent her next move. She said nothing but opened up her beaded purse, took out a bottle of cologne, and started to perfume me. Her fingers about my neck and throat were so insistent that I remember enduring the assault with what must have been an unnerving stillness.

Then it was over. I think I smiled, perhaps a bit coyly, because my aunt's face looked vaguely stern as she knelt and took my shoulders in her hands. Now her touch was calmer, her whole demeanor more thoughtful, but her advice was so obscure and in some ways so alien to my thought I had no trouble dismissing it for years. "Don't think about what they may think," she whispered at my ear. "Old Bear believed all women are like flowers."

Later, I watched her move around the house, touching things. None of her physical parts seemed timed to quite the same rhythm. That was the first I understood of class difference. Not that I cared, but she was beneath us. As my mother explained to my cousin, "Utterly graceless. That cheap scent; those painted eyebrows." My mother meant, obliquely, to instruct. She thought my cousin just as bad. "With that neck," she often said, "out of proportion to that face; that torso too long for those legs."

In five years, at that family's second wedding, still shy but by seventeen more self-absorbed, less capable of shame, I wore a black armband and took care the others knew I was as relieved as they that my unsightly cousin had somehow found a mate; that in spite of my youth, I quite understood and agreed the resolution of her future was more important than the otherwise alarming fact he was a head shorter than she and from another culture. He was Japanese. I spent the better part of the afternoon on the floor with his grandmother, sipping pale green tea while from across the room my own outraged grandmother regarded us, her dim eyes, nearly sightless, judgmental, missing nothing. She was exactly like my mother. They even thought the same. I heard them later by the punch bowl.

"Those Japanese," one said.

"How different things would be," confirmed the other, "if they hadn't killed Flo's true love in the war."

That was in 1967. We had a different war before us then. But if I tied a strip of cloth around my arm, it signified little more than the unconscionable pretense of my generation. Like so many others who waved the same banners, I was woefully naïve about what the world held in store. And on that particular day, the small, hard kernel of injustice I had managed to conceive of was so completely overshadowed by what – love, sex? – that I should not have been surprised to find myself reaching later for the bridal bouquet Abbie tossed straight at her new Oriental niece. In retrospect, the configuration of events at her wedding – crisp autumn weather, sweet smells, oblivion – was identical to that at her mother's, and the effect on me could not have been more similar. How hard it is now for me to imagine myself on those two occasions, and yet under the influence of that same brief ritual, I confess to having twice believed we might be spared. As surely as my mother, her mother and myself wept at the appropriate moment, this is the meaning of weddings: despite my conviction that my future would be brighter than my cousin's, when the time came for Abbie to repeat her marital vows, like all the other women, I silently repeated after her.

II.

IT'S JUST a photograph. You have them in every family. You have the landscapes too: post-daguerreotype beaches, smudged sepia parlors. The portrait in question shows Georgia and Bear beside a rosebush. It is winter and they, like the season, are severe – straight-backed and untouching, as if between them and this final product of the sitting, pride and obstinance prevent a more flattering stance. The way the chemicals have preserved them, they remain without history or depth. Familiarity alone enables us to identify where, in relation to our personal geographies, the picture was taken, and after what pain.

On my mother's side, my grandparents were married on the same block of the city where they bought their first home and raised their four children. But Bear, whose immigrant father farmed contiguous acres of artichokes and strawberries and whose mother wore her hair in braids coiled around her head, made no secret through the years that he was looking for a way out. When it came, he took it on instinct, and though by no means old yet, went to work at once on what would be his second and last home. The war, however, interfered, and by the time everyone's objections had been overcome and materials somehow procured, Bear's solitary retirement haven had undergone a kind of secular transubstantiation, becoming two instead of one, though only Georgia moved there with him. The girls were in college.

Still, Bear had an eye for these things. He bought land on

the most serene inner curve of the Monterey Bay. He built out of the wind, at the base and to the lee side of humped, eucalyptus-covered dunes where a clean and pungent odor tinged the afterscent of fog. Finally, he laid a brick porch between the front doors and covered it with a green, translucent awning so that, from a distance, the two houses gave the appearance of one. The trick here is to imagine two discrete living quarters, each self-contained: kitchen, bath, bedrooms, parlor or den. The real trick is to imagine a family so self-absorbed that its inability to extricate one part from the other is expressed in the houses it lives in. The antithesis of love is not always rejection.

From the city to the country, when a family makes that move, it is a sign of something – dissonance, denial, deliverance. In this case, Georgia was persuaded only because Bear's grief was more overpowering than her own. It was, as I have said, a premature retirement, but the incident that precipitated Bear's decision was the kind which, by its unexpectedness and magnitude, severs every common bond a person shares with others, reconstructing completely what might before have been a plain and ordinary existence.

As it happened, Bear and Georgia married young, kept the Sabbath, and conceived four children: two daughters and two sons. If you drew the family on a piece of paper, it would form an unsteady triangle, with Bear and Georgia near the top, at right angles to each other: he, white-haired and broad-shouldered, half again as tall as she; she, plump in the way of women who ate dainty, sugared cakes throughout the thirties to reassure themselves the world they knew and raised their children in was not at all the same as the one in which they fed cheese sandwiches to transients on the porch each day at noon. Her charity was based on her conviction that faith in the benevolence of her own heart and nature would somehow return the sardines to the bay, as if with her blessing and kind intervention alone would those unhappy times ever pass. In the same way, with her children she felt not responsible but powerful. It's like that in the diagram. You can see the four siblings, lined up along the hypotenuse, but the pose they have struck is ambiguous as they have draped their arms around each other's shoulders and are smiling, but inwardly, deceitfully. The curve of one's arm is the vise of another's; the averted eyes are darker than is possible in real life. At one end the eldest, at the other the youngest each stands with one hand free, limply dangling it. One is farthest from, the other closest to the outstretched parental grasp; but the longer you study the page, the more the opposing faces at the two outer angles, curiously sexless, seem interchangeable.

As children Georgia's daughters were like her — hearty eaters and good-natured, unambivalent; while the boys, by adolescence, were intractable. Kurt stole wine from the cellar. Justin ate his lunch with riffraff off the streets. Imitating them, he let his hair grow. He brought cheap salami to the table and peeled it with unclean hands, biting into it whole. Less impatient than his wife and more optimistic by nature, Bear predicted that in time the lower class would lose its romance. He'd trim his hair, Bear promised; just give him time enough and he would mend his rhetoric and manners. Of course, Georgia tactfully agreed, but what about a European tour, very popular those days? A change of climate in the meantime might advance a change of heart. Instead their son returned from Germany more wild-eyed than ever, bearded and insulting to his father. Kurt encouraged his excess. He brought up good wine from the cellar and baited his brother with charged questions, the answers to which confirmed the family's worst suspicions. But there was nothing to be done. It was as if Justin had somehow been terribly assaulted. All that remained of him now was a despair that so far exceeded the rest of their sensibilities they found themselves powerless to intervene.

Three weeks after he returned, Justin had his twenty-second birthday. It was winter then. The fog was low and gray, and the chill, deliberate, it seemed, and full of malice, ate into everything. Justin had delicate hands. Especially in rage, his thin white fingers moved as if they met resistance everywhere. The others, out of delicacy, avoided looking at them as he talked, following instead the worn cuffs of his sweater, soiled and a little too long. Despite his mother's preference, Justin wore that sweater for his birthday cocktails, which were served promptly at six. Bear offered gin or bourbon. Justin, who had thought it out beforehand, requested a martini, then settled himself in front of the fire and sipped at it with such languid grace that even Georgia felt a little hopeful. Gently, with a strange abstraction, he worked the silver toothpick back and forth between his fingers, saving the pimiento-stuffed olive to suck at the end. And then while Bear was busy icing the second round of drinks, he slipped upstairs discreetly to his mother's pink-toned bedroom and took her pretty, nacre-butted handgun from the gilt-edged vanity and fired at the mirror. Immediately after, a second shot was heard.

WHEN Bear first bought the land, Georgia refused even to go there. Nothing he could do could distract her from what, after Justin's death, became her sole remaining purpose: to bind the others to her out of danger. And Kurt was too much like his brother – a son and close enough in age – not to bear the full brunt of his mother's grief. Marriage was her idea; his only obligation was to choose a wife, a champagne, and a bunga-low where, in the span of two short years, he himself had fathered sons. Paternity, however, as travel with his brother and filial devotion in both cases, did not suit him, and in the end he balked at Little League. On the day he announced his divorce, Georgia said, "Where on the bay?"

"I'm glad," Bear said, "you finally see how much better it is to desist. I'll take you there tomorrow."

But even then Georgia was not ready for what she finally saw, for what she saw was not the beaches near where Bear paced out the foundation, was not the sea and not the wind-swept sand, but rather the expanse of it. "So much space with nothing in it," she said in horror to herself. "The girls will marry. We'll be left alone." To Bear, a little slyly, she said, "Why don't we build twice? Once for us and once for Rose. Adjacent homes for company, with gardens all around and a sun porch in between." Bear thought about it for awhile before deciding the porch should have an awning: Rose was his fa-vorite, and she was fair-skinned. She had also been indulged all her life, a practice that strengthened her will if not her character.

"What do you mean, you're not coming back?" Florence asked her as she packed her bags for college.

"They'll get old, don't you see?" Rose explained. "It's a trap."

However, Bear had not gotten old. Long before that, in his new house, he died. For days afterward my mother's shocked face was mottled and bruised looking. "Daddy's dead. He died already," she kept repeating numbly to no one in particu-lar. "How could that have happened?"

"Intestinal blockage," my father would say. "But don't worry, dear. You're just feeling guilty. I assure you, the sensa-tion will pass."

"Mother can come here." She sounded hopeful.

He decanted brandy, smiling. "But she won't."

And of course she didn't. For Georgia never thought of moving. What she thought was: of her remaining children, which should have the empty house Rose still refused to ac-cept? And though once she might have wanted Kurt, he was now approaching forty and had been changed by his aimless single life from a reasonably attractive man to a fat one, red-

faced and melancholic. Seeing the method of elimination, Flo
found herself without alternatives. The way the family put it,
someone had to live there. I believe Flo said the same thing to
her husband – the first one, the one who, because of his
health, preferred drier climates. But Georgia never thought
too much of that match in the first place. She was the one who
coined it: *a reaction*. "You know," she liked to say, "poor Florence lost her true love in the war."

It is in the nature of families that a single member's failure
frees the others from their own. The nature of this particular
family is that by the time Flo was divorced and Kurt pulled
himself together and proposed to an old high school sweet-
heart, it was too late for them. Soon after they were married,
Kurt collapsed in his green Ford on their way to see a ball
game, caught in traffic across the water from Candlestick Park,
a thermos of martinis in his lap. Florence and Georgia heard
the news with their unerring sense of justice: Betty Sue drank
gin, so they blamed her.

Yet if they reached the same conclusion, they were always at
odds over what to do about it. And if they lived together seven
years, alone except for Abbie, there was no reason to assume
they agreed on the conditions. Georgia took her daughter's
presence for granted but in her heart would surely have preferred the other, Rose. Flo was faithful to her mother, but
privately chafed. So when the third man in her life proposed
she only waited long enough until she was alone before she
called the florist, charging it to Georgia. Several months later,
and just weeks after the Soviets had withdrawn their offending
missiles from Cuba, her second legal husband proved different
from the first only insofar as he could pay for his own whiskey.

But Florence had a daughter now, a witness to her failure,
and Abbie always says it was as slow and as relentless as a
dream. She says she heard shouting, the sound of something
shattering, a dull thump as she made her way across the

porch. Inside, the dark hallway acted like a funnel. Words came down it, brutal and distinct. I have often imagined my cousin with the flats of her palms on either wall for support. She says he only said it once, and at first her confusion was such she thought he must mean her: "Either she goes, or I do," he said, and Florence said nothing.

By the time Abbie figured out he meant Georgia and not her, she had started down the hall. She meant somehow to stop him. Her unexpected insight was her own deliverance, at which her relief was so great that not even her mother's bruised face in the morning could diminish her new and unfamiliar sense of power. She would be the one to stay. It was her house now.

In the end, only Betty interfered, offering the spare room in her duplex, but Georgia insisted on a cottage down the coast from the houses Bear had built. From then until she died more than half a decade later, it was not my aunt Florence, who had committed the offense, but my other aunt Betty Sue whom Georgia could never forgive for the hapless indiscretion by which she had made public what should have been a private matter. And so Georgia moved out by herself to that cottage where the wind swept straight off the ocean and scoured the rough siding gray. Gulls flocked there, littering everything with their filth. The air reeked of kelp. Yet my grandmother was so determined the efforts and expectations of her life should not have been in vain that she refused absolutely to acknowledge the slightest sign of compromise or decline in her condition, and in our never-ending efforts to appease her, we too were forced to participate in the complicated charade that nothing had changed.

Thus, in early adolescence I learned to handle stainless steel flatware as if it were silver. With impeccable manners I ate off cheap stoneware, served by myself from the left. I drank wine out of flat-bottomed glasses more soberly than if they had had

stems. This was difficult, especially for my mother, especially
when her mother's vision started failing and to compensate
the older woman had mirrors installed all over the cottage,
further confusing her struggle with life with so many redun-
dant images. Eventually, nurses were brought in, but they
were hard to find and keep. Georgia would not listen to them.
Georgia would complain that they were rude and dirty. Georgia would dismiss them when no one came to tea.

MY GRANDMOTHER on my mother's side is dead now. She
died slowly of the failure of her senses and without relief from
that humiliation. Her last days were incontinent. They found
her in soiled pajamas. Still, in her heart she hadn't changed,
and I will never forget the grim set of her face at Abbie's
wedding. The force of her condemnation made nothing so
clear as that banishment from her own home and all that
introspection had not in the least changed her view of the
world. One afternoon of familial grace, and already she
couldn't keep from disapproving of what went on in it.

It was in this spirit that she also raised her children. "Blood
all over my bedroom," she told me the last time I saw her.
"How did he dare?" We were then at the height of the Vietnam
War, and the armband, which several years before had been
perceived as an affectation, was now such a familiar part of my
uniform that my grandmother said nothing about it. But her
eyes, vague as they were, accused, examining my face and
dirty denim in such a way as to make me feel ill at ease and not
a little put out. The trip had been an inconvenient detour from
a march in San Francisco. Now, though my sense of obligation
was ingrained deeply enough to keep me there for a decent
interval, I was anxious to return to my friends in the city. As
my grandmother talked, I thought about the clams we would
eat later, and the cold and bitter wine. I anticipated marijuana,
sex. But she was old and I was her daughter's daughter, so I

forced myself to listen despite how her thoughts seemed to wander that day, often beyond the mere vicissitudes of age. What was it she said about her male children: less resilient than the girls? "Be glad you are a girl." She also said, "Survival of the fittest." This was to place the blame for the failure of her children – and through them of her life – squarely on them. She wanted no part of it, and this was understandable. Yet we were both mistaken to place our faith, like that, in absolution.

It was near dusk before I felt free to go, but when I stood to say good-bye, her startled, if unfathomable, expression held me by her bed an instant longer. During our last moments together we exchanged deliberate scrutinies, and I can only assume my own eyes reflected the same unspeakable distrust and tenderness as hers. But neither of us was quite prepared to play a conciliatory role. Instead of offering her dry, soft cheek for me to kiss, she turned petulantly away and groped along her nightstand. Even through the sweet, medicinal taint of the room I could smell kelp. Concentrating on that, I found the pills she wanted and placed them firmly in her hand, but at my touch her face altered and her whole body seemed to recoil in a shock of recognition. Then, sucking in her lower lip, she delivered this final message to me: "You? You're not even married yet, are you?"

In the intervening years since then I have found what I'm unable to forget is not the sight of Georgia spent against her yellowed pillow just days before she died, but rather the puzzling tone of her dismissal. I didn't know then and I still can't say if she spoke with contempt, or envy.

III.

I was, in the days before my aunt's wedding, a shy, imaginative child, inquisitive, yet intensely vulnerable. As a result small things loomed disproportionately large in my perception: an unjust word, the single blue heron that nested every summer of my childhood in the brackish marshland at the edge of Bear's land. That bird in particular I remember as a stately, haunting shadow I used to watch for, for hours, unsubstantial and elusive in the fog. So yes, there was about Aunt Florence's contingent of the family some vague, unsettling thing that made the dank coastal world they inhabited seem charged with a disquieting energy. As we approached along the highway we passed horse pastures, vegetable stands, and a small, white-markered cemetery, littered with religious tracts and artificial flowers. More disquieting still was the queer configuration of the houses themselves – the triptych-like image they imposed on the surrounding landscape, with the porch the very center of the center panel. Eastward from there gardens, dunes, and sky formed a series of vertical blocks, while to the west the flat, uncompromising earth always seemed to me to be as close to heaven as a person might come in this life – not ascension, but one long horizontal brush out to the sea. Like my mother, however, I instinctively preferred closer spaces and thus associated the conflict I felt during our visits with my aunt's lush gardens, threatening even in retrospect but never so much as when they still provided Mother with an unmediated focal point for all her petty jealousy and guilt. She has since discovered the vindication of houseplants. I, in contrast, have been overwhelmed by the compulsion to identify our real source of dread.

As a child, nothing focused my uneasiness as completely as the hummingbirds that swarmed among the crimson bugles of Flo's fuchsias. What I felt for those birds – love, maybe – was so profound and yet irrational that whenever we arrived, my first impulse was to take my cousin's butterfly net from where it lay neglected among spider webs and mulch and go after my tormentors with a single-mindedness of purpose the rest of the family mistook for enthusiasm. It was never possible to catch the birds, but I would often watch from close enough to see the quick, needlelike probe of their tongues, the only discernible movement throughout the long, hovering caesuras in which they took their sustenance. In retrospect, I think their stillness must somehow have frightened me, for I remember unconsciously mimicking it until we were caught in a single instant of uncanny harmony and I lashed out wildly, intent not on their frail, arched wingspans but on the distances that separated me from them, suddenly immense. I wanted always to control the incomparably brutal rush of their flight. More than anything I wanted not to be surprised by it, ever.

And so it was inevitable that my obsessive hunt should eventually lead back behind the other house, where one August afternoon and quite by accident I discovered the unnatural bedroom my grandmother and aunt kept exactly as it was when Bear lived there. Its existence confused my objective, and now I often felt myself drawn from my original pursuit to the window, densely shrouded with azaleas, I had found. Thus, on the pretense of studying nature, I slipped discreetly through the thorny branches to press close against the glass and observe, unobserved, the room I then believed Bear and other pale giants used by night. The bed was three times broader than my own, and much higher. The burnished copper hood above the fireplace was large enough for eucalyptus limbs. The stones of the hearth rose as high as my chest.

If you are a true believer in weddings, if you cannot conceive of the ceremony without a blue garter and a piece of old lace, you must know that the ritual of union is in fact the first intimation of death in every married person's life. At twelve I would never have believed that, for my future lay before me. But Betty did. Only Betty, who would later behave with greater decency than all of us combined, could embrace the essential ambiguity of hope; yet our resistance to her was so strong we were unwilling even to acknowledge the benevolence and grace of that acceptance.

For myself, it would be years before I thought to compare the red paint on her nails, the quick and fragile movement of her hands about my throat as she performed her trite, but generous, baptism of cologne, with the straight dark stocking seams down the backs of Aunt Flo's rigid calves, and still several more years before I found the latter wanting. I mean that as a girl and well into adulthood I remained not only willing, but anxious to betray fulfillment for wishes. Even now, having passed beyond that time of ripeness in my life — more politely known as the brief interval in which a girl is first desirable, and later simply eligible — I can still remember how that unfamiliar scent on me smelled faintly like gardenias throughout the ceremony, and as bright and as cheap as a promise. But of course I had no way of knowing then that under the threat of war or matrimony everything seems lush and full for awhile.

Wait Until Heaven

I. FRAN

Fʀᴀɴ wants to begin by asking for your patience. This won't be easy for any of us and she has some concern that too many people are involved, too many generations. But what's to be done? Families are never smoothly disentangled from themselves, and though Fran would like to think in smaller terms, would like to look out from where they're seated at the breakfast nook table, through the paned and polished window, to the twisted, gray-limbed plum tree and think of nothing more than the erratic flight of bluejays at the glass and aluminum bird feeder Cilla sent for Christmas not two months before that hangs from the third left branch, the table itself keeps reminding her of certain material facts which, fixed, determine this and any other configuration of events she might unfold.

For instance: that the table, heavy oak, once had been painted the same pale cucumber green the fourth corner back claw foot still remains, and that finally, after suffering the hateful color for years, in a rage at thirty-one, Fran had gone ahead and stripped it. It took her three months, beginning in

June and all through the hottest season to the first dreary autumn after Cilla had married. She worked out in back in direct valley sun, sweating through and staining long-sleeved shirts.

"I said I'd do it, and now I'm doing it," she told her mother.

"Wear your bathing suit at least," her mother said. "You always tan so nicely."

Fran put on jeans instead, thinking with each hard rasp of the sandpaper that at last her sister had deserted her. When she came to the fourth scalloped foot and left it green, suddenly her rage subsided.

Or for instance this: that across the teak-floored dining room and down the grass-clothed hall in the bedroom with the marble fireplace, Fran's grandmother, Ida, having taken morphine not that day or the one before but some time the previous night, lies stretched beneath the feather quilt on the old, high, narrow bed as she slips even now ever closer to death with a yellowed photograph of her late husband, Chester, pinned to the inside of her nightdress.

And that's the next thing. Fran wishes there were other ways of telling this without hurting anyone (change the occasion to a birthday party, renegotiate the relationships), but because in her head she wants nothing more than that it be over, she also knows that everything depends on what is included, and how. All or nothing, she's begun to think, by which she means the strictest, most honest attention to detail – to the undercast of every color, as well as the apparent hue, to what is absent just as much as what is present. In other words, Fran's grandfather has been dead now a quarter of a century, she hasn't seen her father since she was seven, and the same goes for Walt, only Fran was thirty-one when she left him, the last time, in Las Vegas. That was twenty-two months ago exactly and, until she called two nights before, also the last time Fran had talked to her sister. Louis alone remains, whom

Fran did meet one time when he was still a poor artist and Cilla was still a poor student and they both still pretended disinterest in settling down. They had dined, the three of them, in Massachusetts, on red pepper pasta and cheap chianti. Six months later Louis was awarded his first grant, and six months after that Cilla was awarded her degree, and six weeks after that they were married.

One final note about the bluejays: the feeder is designed for smaller birds – chickadees, warblers. Jays cannot land on the tiny perches. So they squawk and dive, squawk and dive, scaring off finches as Fran and Cilla (who cares nothing about any of this, which is her mistake for surely she will in time) watch from the breakfast nook table.

W E W E R E sitting at the breakfast nook table having coffee and staring grimly out beyond the muddied river to red hills sparsely clotted with buckbush, Digger pine, and manzanita. It was raining. Closer in, late red and pink camellias pressed against the window; early cream-colored narcissus fringed the neglected back lawn. Neither of these – not the yard and not the hills – was identical to the world Cilla had so covetously taken in from the portable steps of the small prop jet she arrived on the previous night, but near enough that no one who saw both would believe the bored superior expression she wore now. She had naturally expected a quick neat funeral, then back to Louis, her sharp, vain sculptor. I'm not being critical. Once I loved my sister absolutely and without reservation. Now all I can say is that after almost two years, the sound of Mother weeping in the back bedroom seemed as audible and calculated as it must at times have seemed to Father, but Cilla didn't hear it that way.

I was, as usual, wearing faded denims. Cilla, in hose though it was morning, had on the navy wool skirt she had worn on the plane and a starched pinstriped blouse but not the suit jacket. The brandy in my coffee wasn't helping much either. Cilla's a shrink — "psychologist," as she used to correct me. In any case, she has a way of making things difficult. Now every so often she'd glance at me sideways as if to let me know that though I might hold her responsible for everything, she most certainly was not. "Blame Walt, if you have to blame someone," she would have said if I had asked her, so I didn't. That was between Walt and me and went back to the May night in Las Vegas when he lost all his money and I told him I was through with gambling.

"You don't even play," he had said. "You just watch."

"I mean you, dear," I told him, "my one gamble in life. And it didn't pay off." Then I called Cilla.

"Louis says," she said, "you're welcome to visit. Fran, visit, he says."

I stared out our hotel window to the neon-tainted night and tried to imagine trees where Cilla was, three thousand miles distant, just leafing out. Spring depresses me anyway. Walt was already asleep so I studied his reflection in the glass — left hand wedged beneath his hip, right leg flung loosely across the geometric-patterned spread — until my sister disconnected me.

I packed, but Walt didn't wake up. I kissed his forehead, which was cool, but still he slept. It was always like that, his forehead was — cool — from the first night he came upon me in Montana. I was camped out alone by one of those green glacial lakes where whenever you hear noises at night you think of bears. And then Walt stepped into the circle of my fire. He was wearing a plaid flannel shirt, unbuttoned, and a pair of old green Can't Bust 'Ems. In his army knapsack he had a few unmatched socks, a ragg sweater, and three spiral notebooks. That was all. But he told me he'd been hiking those trails since June, living off berries and fish. When I asked where he slept, he spread my down bag on a beach of black pebbles. Later he explained the notebooks were because he was a poet which, after I read through them, I never doubted. Even on those hottest August afternoons his forehead remained startlingly cool.

But without Walt I couldn't go back to Montana from Vegas and Louis wouldn't have me in the east, so I had no choice but to turn west again, back to California where my mother and my grandmother continued to insist on the long-standing pretense of affection that had been the emotional staple of my childhood. I took a midnight bus. And yes, I kept telling myself the whole way, among the crying babies and between the endless twenty-minute stops, it, my retreat, was only temporary, a breathing space during which I could decide my next move, reconstruct events at any rate in order to convince myself Walt had waked at the last minute and whispered that he loved me. But he hadn't.

Sometime the next morning the desert changed to mountains I had crossed the first time years before with my mother and my sister on another west-bound bus. Cilla cried much of the way. Three years older, I was more self-controlled. Besides, I meant to call my father as soon as we arrived to tell him where we'd gone and have him come and get me. But I didn't know about long-distance in those days. By the time I had saved the right number of coins, the number I dialed was no longer in service.

My mother and my grandmother were waiting on the front porch when I pulled up in the taxi.

My mother said, "I knew he'd never marry you. He's not the marrying type."

My grandmother said, "Now Ruth, I warned you. Fran's here for a rest. She needs a rest. You leave Fran to me."

I was thinking that was just what she had said to my grandfather when the three of us arrived all those years before from Colorado. My grandfather hadn't lasted long. The way I under-

stood it, that was his decision. He could have had his guts cut
out, sewn up and put back in, but he preferred to die with
dignity and whiskey.

"Who could blame him?" I used to tell Walt. "Four women
all at once, and one of them Ida."

As for Cilla, I knew I couldn't blame her deference to her
husband either, but I did. That was how it always was between
us. What she had learned in her schools to call *sibling rivalry*, I
had always called *how sisters love each other*. Cilla, for example,
had boyfriends, but I never did. Cilla also had career goals,
while I had a tendency to wander from interest to interest,
state to state, trying out landscapes as they presented themselves to me, trying not always to define where I was by the
distance between me and Walt. Walt, who came later, wasn't
really a boyfriend, and in any case with him it was never very
steady. It was steady with Cilla, from the earliest beginning,
from Colorado even, her and me, both self-absorbed, both
passionately engaged in circumnavigating the elaborate paths
of the other's life, thereby hemming her in, achieving dominance. If I marched against the war in San Francisco, Cilla
screwed a poet. And so on, until the sixties ended.

"You're all out of causes," Cilla accused.

"Under the circumstances why bother with causes?"

"What circumstances?"

"If you have to ask there's no use explaining. But don't
worry, Cilla. It doesn't matter."

"Nothing matters, then?"

"More or less."

Which was, more or less, what Walt said about that time
when, all out of causes himself, he gave in and allowed the
kind of life he had been living now since he finished college — poker, cheap beer, and no more poetry — had not
panned out as he had gambled. Walt was depressed. Walt was
getting fat. Walt needed, Walt wrote: *a woman to see to my needs*.

There's no one in Montana. I've looked. You'll do. Come north.

"And like an animal conditioned to respond, you'll respond?" Cilla said.

"Do I have choices? What are my choices?"

"Go back to school. Get a job. Come live with me."

We were sitting at the breakfast nook table, still cucumber green, the last time we were home together before she left for grad school. In the next room Mother and Ida — not yet but almost blind and increasingly incontinent — had been arguing all morning. Occasionally their voices rose: *"That's not true, Mother. We all love you. The girls adore you."*

"I know they want their independence, but does she have to go three thousand miles away to get it? You never went that far, and you never went long."

Cilla picked up Walt's postcard again, the one with a prospector's corpse being eaten by vultures. "That's some invitation," she said. "But you're not really going, Fran. I can't believe you're really going."

"At least she's doing something with her life. That's more than you can say about her sister."

I went. And left and went and left and went, like some volcano-surprised bird so dazed by the ash I could never quite get my directions straight, or one of the myriad floundering insects whose wings left tiny trailings in the grit. But the ash never fell on us until we'd been at it more years than I will ever care to count and I don't know. Walt's gambling was beside the point. The point was: I wasn't light enough, I wasn't dark enough. I tucked in top sheets, buttered sandwiches, burned off-white utility candles. As a girl I'd deserted my father, a musician. Now I played no instrument at all: what was wrong with me? What the hell was wrong with Fran?

By the time Mt. St. Helens did erupt, I welcomed the corrosive fallout as just the right shroud for yet another spring. Walt and I watched the sulfuric cloud bring an acid yellow dusk down three hours early. Then he put on a white gauze surgical mask and went out. Four hot, windless days later, it rained, the roads reopened, and we decided to try our luck in Vegas.

Meanwhile, Cilla had pursued a strict course of self-improvement: taking on her academic duties and meeting them with high distinction, taking on the most challenging clients who made the most remarkable recoveries, taking on the occasional gifted lover and then at just the right moment breaking off the affair with no hard feelings on either side, finally taking on Louis. Her timing had never been better.

Five days later, long-distance, she said, "I'm sorry to hear that, but I'm married now, Fran."

"But you always said if I ever needed anyplace to go."

"Louis's my husband."

"You've never loved anyone in your life, have you?"

"I said you were welcome to visit," she said.

California was the opposite direction, where in the intervening two years I had learned to bathe my grandmother with a soft flannel cloth and to diaper her discreetly, never pricking flesh. I had also learned to mix martinis by the pitcher, one for each of us so we could sleep.

Well of course we drank. We had to because of all those years we spent together, sometimes four women, sometimes two, now three, and each with her own motive for hatred, the one because she left the man she bore two daughters by in order that her mother might have company for tea, the other because the man she had been married to for more than fifty years refused to have his surgery while his daughter was around to see what it would do to him. And so he died but she didn't, my grandmother didn't. No, Ida lived on for many years, tying pink bows at my and Cilla's backs, instructing us on Shakespeare and on how to cross our legs. She further was insistent that we light the wicks of candles before we put them out, iron parallel folds in the linen towels, and distrust any sign of affection from a man. It was always so easy for Ida that way. One call to Colorado and (never mind about our father who was out that night, as he was every other, playing his flat-backed mandolin for our supper): *Yes, Mother, of course, Mother, we'll be right there, Mother.* By some complex calculations of hers, he'd lost his right to us anyway. She said as much herself that single time he called two or three years later when she told him if he ever did again she'd have him tracked down and arrested. We were all listening. She hung up before Mother even knew what had happened. But yet I, too, had said my catechism, and the truth of it is the way things turned out, just like my mother before me, I left the only man I've loved since I've been old enough to know what that should mean because my grandmother went blind and my mother cried on the telephone and my man lost his money in Las Vegas and my sister, a shrink who should have known better, deserted me for a system of ethics I don't understand and a man who sculpts the contours of her back while she is sleeping.

Cilla was sleeping when I called to tell her what Ida had done. Her voice after two years sounded high and very distant. I said what I had to say. Three thousand miles away I could hear the rustling of her down comforter.

Then she said, "Who have you called?"

"No one," I said.

"I'll be there tomorrow," she said. "Call someone right now."

What the hell. We always knew about the morphine — inside the old fur muff that smells of camphor, inside the I. Magnin's pink hatbox, on the top closet shelf above plastic-wrapped furs — which eventually she got down and took. But it must have been stale. That's what we found so intolerable, really: not that she took it, but that it was stale.

After awhile I got up to put more brandy in my coffee.

"Is that brandy you're putting in your coffee?" Cilla said.

I smiled at her from across the table. Professional life had aged her much more than my erratic habits had me, but she cultivated it too, with that strict high thrust to her shoulders and that tasteful pinstriped shirt. She didn't smile back.

"We really should," she said, "call someone, you know."

"Did you have anyone in mind? Louis? Walt, maybe?" I paused. This would hurt her. "Daddy?"

I was waiting for her answer when Mother walked through to the kitchen. We exchanged glances, but I wasn't going in there, not to the back bedroom with the marble fireplace, never again as far as I was concerned. If my grandmother was dying, she made that choice herself and good for her. After the betrayal of her family came the betrayal of her body: what was left for her? Or put it another way: Ida had lost power, so Ida took it back the only way she knew. This final time, however, she had miscalculated. Still, everything was changed by what she'd done — Cilla's sidelong glances at me, our disparate perceptions of the rain — and certainly we would have preferred that it be otherwise. We would have preferred to be stripped, like the table, of our pasts. But Mother, in the next room, was rummaging among bottles and we knew she would never let us forget.

Almost more than anything I regretted the melodrama. There were pills she had asked for often enough I could have given her that would have been quicker at least. Or two years back if I had gone home to Montana by myself, maybe Mother would have cried on the telephone to Cilla. Her marriage was new. What could Louis have done if she had called it off? Unfortunately, in those days I believed that while a person's options may never seem the same in retrospect, once you've made the first decision the rest is predetermined: you budget your long-distance calls, but you pay your telephone bill; you keep the hatbox or you throw it away. I used to believe that. Now I wanted to be wrong. I wanted to think that with nothing more than another shot of brandy or a pack of imported cigarettes I could alter the configuration of the family altogether, switch siblings, allegiances, rack Cilla with guilt, absolve Mother.

But no, I told myself, sticking to the facts: morphine it was and would remain. The table was oak, with one remaining green foot. My sister's hose had no unsightly runs. Louis would call before long. And Walt, forget about Walt. Walt was just a signifier anyway. I'd never see Walt again.

II. CILLA

FRAN and I had been sitting in the little breakfast area off the dining room, hardly talking, almost all day when Ruth joined us with what could not have been her first drink that day, a double martini but without any olives. I'm assuming it was not her first because she put her glass down on the table rather clumsily, saying as she did, "Girls..." and the "i" sounded more like a heavily flattened "u." Her glass was an exquisite long-stemmed cocktail glass I remembered Chester drinking from, but with one chip now at the rim. There might have been some small bit of blood on Ruth's lip. Somewhere back behind the flowering plum another angry jay screeched.

"For years," Fran said, "they tormented us. Now we torment them."

I picked up Ruth's drink and wiped off the ring it had left, but before putting it back on a silk-screened place mat I'd sent her for one occasion or another, I heard myself saying, "It's over, she's dead then," and took three deep swallows of what must have been almost straight gin, very little vermouth.

No one said anything for a minute, but Fran looked at me as if, once again, I'd betrayed her by stating the obvious. Ruth blotted first her lip, then her eyes, though they were dry. Death seemed so anticlimactic under the circumstances. I felt tired and I wanted to change into something more comfortable but had, as usual, packed lightly. If it had been anyone else I wouldn't have hesitated about borrowing something loose and intimate. With Fran, though, and after two years, even asking for Levis sounded vaguely improper.

"Don't be an ass," she said. "I've got lots. They're in the drawer." She paused. "But don't you think we should call someone now?" Seconds later, from the bedroom, I could hear her at Ruth: "Are you sure? You've got to be sure."

Fran was like that from as long as I remember, not deliberately hard so much, sometimes, as just stubborn. She'd steal from Ida's gardens to have camellias for her armbands. She'd insinuate love and then hold out her own alienation like some kind of banner. Fran was big on banners, most flowers, and war casualty figures. Her tirades were painful. Often I wanted nothing more than that she'd desist. But if it wasn't the war, it was the inane pretensions of our social class. If it wasn't that, it was *Power to the people*. Neither Ruth nor Ida nor I knew quite what *people* she had in mind, but she was very passionate about them. My dates thought so too. Some nights we never made it to the movie or dance or whatever we'd arranged. Some nights they'd leave, much later than I ever kept them out, with one of Fran's stolen camellias firmly anchored in their buttonholes or hooked behind their ears. There was such bitterness in her and it came in the most attractive guises and I loved her so intensely I would have abdicated anything to her self-righteousness if she had asked it of me. But she never did.

Her jeans were too tight, so I tried another pair, which were also too tight but which zipped instead of buttoned, and I forced them closed. After all that brandy she had switched to gin. That seemed like a good idea to me too.

Ruth said, "You've put on weight."

"I lead a sedentary life," I said.

"You should exercise," she said. "Look at me. I swim."

"Are you going to call?" Fran said. "Or shall I?" When I said nothing she got up and dialed a number. "A heart attack, yes," Fran said coolly on the phone. "Yes. Lately she'd been having trouble with her heart."

"It wasn't as if we could have done anything else," Ruth was saying to me. "You have to think what Ida wanted. You have to imagine what it's been like for her."

"Mother," Fran said. "Cilla, put her to bed."

It was four o'clock in the afternoon, still raining, but the clouds had lifted a little and it was lighter out than before. At the horizon, faintly, and beyond the red hills, I could see blue. Even under those particular circumstances it was an unreasonable bedtime, but not to Fran, who got up and took Ruth off herself when she finished her drink.

Then I was alone, and somewhat surprised to find myself thinking how I wanted to be strong. Not for my mother and not that I no longer cared what she thought of me either – or I of her – though I didn't very much. But the time had long passed since my mother had been able to rub my back and soothe me about Fran, and I, as a result, had been calling her Ruth now for years and sending cryptic postcards instead of long intimate letters. Whereas Fran still wasn't talking to me, even long-distance. So it was for her that I wanted to be strong, for once, though if we kept drinking as heavily as we seemed to promise to, I suspected that was going to be difficult.

The phone rang and she got it in the hall, next to the open doorway where she stood and watched me as she talked. She answered distinctly, deliberately, after which there was a longish pause. Then she said, "And you've got dirty socks." Walt? I thought, curious. "But you don't understand," she went on. "I don't think she wants to."

"Mother safely off to bed?" I asked when she hung up.

"I gave her some Valium for after the alcohol wears off."

"Fives?"

"I don't think so. They were blue."

The odd thing is she was right. I really didn't want to talk to Louis just then. All my training to the contrary, I had believed as much as anyone that as soon as we were married I could forget who I had been and start out fresh. Louis actually encouraged my delusion. It was the only thing he was ever consistent about. No matter what I said, he always said, "I don't want to hear about your past." I took that like the rest, a relief really, at least in the beginning when it seemed we loved each other with such an overriding passion that whatever we didn't share in common could mean nothing. By the time I figured out that only worked one way, I had given up too much to get it back.

Fran, of course, saw how things were at once, straight to the heart of them, quick and sharp. She had made it back east between moves to Montana and was cooking dinner, some kind of spaghetti, hot with crushed chili. Louis brought red wine. They were getting along quite nicely. Fran's face was flushed and, I thought, exceptionally pretty. She was even laughing about Walt, about some poker game he'd insisted she come to and then kept getting drawn out on until he tried to place her for his bet. She told it as if it were funny. Louis said he'd like to have been one of the players. "Not you," Fran said. "Daddy."

"Our father?" I said.

"You know, the man who played the mandolin and made you cry."

"You saw him?"

"No, but Walt thought it might be. That's why he brought me along. There was this man, see, passing through with this banjo..."

"I meant what I said," Louis interrupted her. And then he left, though it was not yet ten o'clock. Fran looked at me so I told her. I said, "He doesn't like to hear about our past."

In those days we used jelly jars for glasses. Fran's was half full. She contemplated it briefly before finishing it in successive swallows. She said, "Well I guess a person makes concessions for artists."

As for marrying Louis in order to extricate myself from my family and make good the three thousand miles I had managed to put between them and me, that worked, but not as I expected. The night Fran called from Las Vegas my husband and I argued bitterly. Even after everything I couldn't see what harm it would do for Fran to live with us for awhile if that's what she needed. She was my sister, after all, but Louis would rather have put up a client of mine, one of those Vietnam vets who still wakes in the middle of the night grabbing for something at his side. "What," I asked him several times a week. "Find out what, and it will disappear." Not really believing my own self, I nevertheless emphasized the word *disappear*. He clawed through the cover of his mattress, gouging his fingers on the springs. Louis didn't get the veteran – he got the bed instead and used it in a sculpture. And I didn't get Fran.

Two nights before when she had called she'd sounded just the same, as if she would still do what she could and had to – was doing it right then, making the unpleasant call – but remained fundamentally surprised that life should turn out as it had, should present such queer and unnecessarily difficult problems for her negotiation. Even now the irregular arch of her eyebrows, the way she had her chin propped in cupped palms, head angled slightly, and was looking out toward the unfortunate bird feeder that had been so pretty in the Cambridge shop – all that – there was something of a startled look about her, fragile and more vulnerable than I'd seen in the past, and so much less of the thwarted jay.

Because I had to say something I said, "It's funny, Fran, but one day when I was, oh, about fifteen I woke up for some reason thinking how I no longer wanted to grow up and be like Ruth.''

''I don't think that's funny,'' Fran said. ''I never wanted that.''

''That's not the funny part. I wanted to grow up and be like you.''

She got up for more gin – a pitcher this time – and while she was crushing the ice, I thought of everything I'd done to be admired – ironed my panties, forced food down the throats of exquisite anorexics, married an artist. I didn't want ice. I wanted gin straight, smooth and hot down my own throat that had resisted such indulgence all those nights I had to be sober in case one of my clients might call. Before that, there was the practicum, and before that, classes, exams. It was hard, but I'd done well for myself, much the better of the two of us. And yet contrition is an act of will, and I was still the one to feel guilty.

Fran came back carrying two frosted glasses and the frosted pitcher. She seemed pleased with herself. She said, ''Well, I guess that's that for Ida. We won't be seeing Ida again.''

''Don't worry,'' I said. ''You'll get used to that.''

She turned to me sharply. ''Is that what you tell your clients?''

I turned just as sharply, away, saying, ''Of course not...'' but thinking that was how it was with families: having once been spurned, you spurn in return, back and forth and over and over, until this: ''I tell them to wait until heaven.''

In Massachusetts, the night Fran made the pasta, Louis came back after she fell asleep. ''Did he really play banjo?'' he asked. That was the extent of our reconciliation, just enough to make me see my lover in a new way, his clay-spattered coveralls, his worn turquoise T-shirt. ''Cerulean,'' he corrected me, but all I could think was how handsome he was, more so by far than any man I'd ever hoped to have, handsomer even than Walt, whom I despise. Especially his hands – long, thin fingers, gaunt wrists – overwhelmed me. Fran has hands like that, the fingers at least, and for years she had begged for a guitar, for a piano, while privately I had been glad each time Ida assured her how much she'd hate to practice, how she'd get bored, how she would give it up. "Now if Cilla were interested," Ida said, but I knew my limitations. That's one of the things Louis came to admire in me: my clients improve but slowly, my stockings don't run but they're mesh, not sheer.

When Fran spoke again, it was softly, and without any of her previous rancor. She sounded a little puzzled, but also resolved. She said, "For so long I found it so easy to disparage you, what you did. You grated Louis's carrots. You made those extraordinary Szechuan pickles. And you chose a profession in which you instruct people on how not to suffer, as if suffering weren't in the nature of things. Meanwhile, in Montana, I went to country bars in cowboy boots and danced. Do you know what I mean?"

I didn't. "Why are you telling me this?"

"You're the shrink. You tell me." After awhile she went on, "We had a second-floor apartment that looked out on a school for exceptional children – dwarfs, paraplegics, mental deficients. Some mornings when Walt still hadn't come home from the night before, I'd sit and watch them play. They had trouble doing the normal things – running, playing catch – but if their ball went over the fence and into the street, they stumbled after it, oblivious to danger, and if one of them fell, they all went down in affectionate imitation. Watching them, what I used to think about was how I'd like to take them dancing. I wanted that we should all have our own instruments – banjos, guitars, and yes, mandolins. I wanted that we should play them and that we should dance."

"Did Walt," I said when she paused, "do that often, stay out all night?"

"Damn it, Cilla. That isn't the point. This is your profession and you still miss every point."

"I'm sorry. Let's go back. What *was* the point?"

"One day the ash came. For twelve hours the air was dense and sulfuric. When it cleared, everything was gray and the children were gone. Walt went out after them."

"Are you drunk? You're not making any sense. You must be drunk."

"I had nothing left to offer them, that's all I mean to say, not Walt and not those pathetic children. As soon as the town reopened, we went to Las Vegas. When I called, you had nothing left to offer me."

Outside the rain had almost stopped and the flowers, weighted down all afternoon with accumulated water, were rising just in time to meet the dusk. What Fran had just said, maybe she was right. Ash I knew nothing about; but I'd thought I'd understood my sister and me. Now I wasn't sure. It still hurt too much.

I said, "Do you remember when we left Colorado?"

Fran picked up her glass. "You cried."

"And you wandered up and down the bus, talking to strange men. *Do you know where we're going*, you asked them. *If you see my daddy, let him know.*"

"They must never have seen him," she said. "But that doesn't matter now, you know that."

"Oh? Then nothing matters."

"Haven't we been through this before?"

"Walt. What about Walt?"

Fran finished her drink and got up to stand by the window, but closed her eyes: what was it she saw? "Walt especially doesn't matter," she said finally. "I used to think he did. I lived here for two years thinking that he did. But whether you have a man or not, either way you're on your own. Believe me. Look at Ida. A quarter of a century later and she dies with a photograph of Chester pinned to the inside of her nightdress. Think of that photograph, Cilla."

Instead I got up to stand beside her. We were exactly the same height and I leaned my head against her shoulder. She didn't move away, but she didn't put her arm around me either. "It wasn't easy," I said, "trying to be like you. I had to screw poets. I had to pretend the war mattered. I didn't know how much it did until now, and now I can't make myself care."

Fran turned to clear the table, moving with decision, as if suddenly sober. She didn't even stop to drain the glasses. I did. And then I poured off the rest of the pitcher and finished that too while she stood in the doorway and watched. We were looking at each other, perfectly aware, so I'll never forget the slight lift of her shoulders, the deliberate half smile, and then what she said before turning to go check on Mother, these words, uttered distinctly: "You can't win grace by willpower alone. Haven't you figured that out by now?"

CILLA isn't happy about ending here, with nothing settled and everything remaining hopelessly ambiguous, but she also has her training and knows things will work out in time. They'll come for Ida before the night is out. Mourning will officially begin. There will be arrangements and then a funeral, not tomorrow or the next day, but probably early the next, quick but not hasty, irreproachably decorous. By then the weather will have cleared and the day they bury Ida will dawn bleak and blue. Perhaps the plum will have blossomed as it does sometimes overnight. Cilla's not sure. She is fairly certain, though, about the dress her sister will be wearing – that old black beaded sheath Fran picked up during college at Goodwill. Cilla herself will wear navy wool. And they'll have coffee early, she and Fran together, once again at the breakfast nook table. Even now, a little later that same afternoon, Fran has already switched to coffee and that bothers Cilla a little, for

Cilla is capable of finding betrayal in anything now.

"What is it," she says, "you said about the bluejays?" Fran doesn't answer. Cilla tries again. "I don't understand why you went to all the trouble of stripping this table. It was such a pretty green that made me think of mint, smell mint, taste mint as we ate our roast lamb."

"Cucumber," says Fran (who suddenly no longer cares about any of this because finally it is time for her to care about something else: a place in Montana, perhaps, not a town and not a wilderness, just a place by the side of the road where, if you settle long enough, the people at the grocery three miles down the road will know you by your first name but never by your lover and certainly not your grandmother, and where yes, wild geese will fly south in the autumn, returning in spring, graceful, "V" 'd markers of all those years to come as she gets up. "So paint it if you don't like it. Match the foot." Then she takes her coffee into the garden where she stands looking out toward the hills.

Alone, suddenly there are things Cilla doesn't want to think about. It shows a certain wisdom that she would rather concentrate on the present moment—the passing into dusk, the last persistent cry of a jay—but her imagination resists her with alarming independence.

For instance: Cilla knows it won't go well at the funeral. As clearly as if it has already taken place, she sees herself and Fran standing by Ida's open grave. Still damp from the night before, the unnaturally manicured cemetery lawn parts around them as it parts around the dead. Several officials are standing around. Ruth doesn't seem to notice them, or anything, for she has been sedated and sits calmly in a black folding chair. And what's that Fran has—a white rose? No, just a camellia. Soon she'll toss it into the grave and they'll leave. It will be over. But, and Cilla knows this, Fran's dress, which glints immodestly in the sun, is too old and perhaps a little too tight.

As Fran raises her hand in a final calculated gesture to her grandmother, the fabric will rip. Beads will scatter. Almost, Cilla can hear them now, their faint clattering on the coffin an unwelcome promise for her future.

Nor does Cilla want to think what Fran will save for their own end. Will she show Cilla where to find the brandy? Will she shrug and say, "So take care of Mother. Take care of yourself if you can, but I doubt it?" Or will she simply ask what Cilla plans?

"Me?" Cilla would say in that case. "You're going, I'm staying, of course."

"But you can't stay here. There's nothing here for you."

"Oh that," Cilla says. "We'll see about that."

Mostly, though, Cilla doesn't like to remember how it was the night before, her first in California. She had jet lag but still hardly slept at all, dozing and starting fitfully until dawn. It wasn't guilt, she wouldn't have called it that, but an anxious feeling, a feeling of utter displacement, the strangest thing. Always, there was the sound of Ruth crying down the hall, sounding more plaintive and alone than anything Cilla had ever heard before, even, she thought, at the hospital. And there was Fran in the next bed, sleeping the way she had when they were children – knees to chest, head folded like a bird's beneath one arm. More than once during the night Cilla had to stop herself from getting up and climbing in with her sister.

Now through the dim light, Cilla can just make out the shadow of the bird feeder, abandoned finally now that the jays have taken roost. Torment, that's what Fran had said: *We torment them.* But surely, Cilla thinks, that isn't necessary. For if she can paint the table, she can take the feeder down. She'll send it back to Louis, who liked it. Did he like it? She does remember buying it in the city from a man who said something about songbirds. Because it's been years since Cilla has paid any proper attention to birds, she's forgotten their names, but

she assumes there must be some in Massachusetts. She wonders if they'll come to Louis's window, if he'll sculpt them.
Perhaps as he does he will remember the curve of her back,
how it used to arch serenely while she slept. But Cilla, who
has never seen her own back from that angle, does not think
of this. The true thing is, having been mercifully distracted,
from now until Fran comes to say, "They're here for Ida," Cilla
doesn't think of anything at all. For now she mustn't.

"Thanks," she tells Fran, and already a certain languid wear-
iness has entered her voice. "Thanks," she repeats. "I'll take
care of it."

Recently I've Discovered My Mistake

I.

Wʜᴇɴ the ash came, it came not as we remembered it most vividly, but as a premature and inauspicious dusk. At first we took the sudden twilight for a storm, except there wasn't any thunder. Instead, a stillness so profound descended on us it was as if that strange cloud had generated itself spontaneously out of the sweet spring air. Minute by minute it thickened, changing from a light, almost delicate amber, to a bilious yellow and finally to a swirling, impenetrable dun.

In the morning we woke to a world unlike any we had ever known. Green, spring-infested hills – made greener just the day before by two weeks of dreary May rain and the memory of a long Montana winter – had been encrusted overnight with the dull cinder. Closer in, the corrosive ash, finer than silt and stinking of sulfur, was the pale gray of sun-bleached bone – black washed to within three shades of white. It smeared everything. New leaves, heavily clotted, drooped or sagged back along branches. Our single row of tulips opened ashen centers to an equally ashen sky. Birds flew in low, dazed circles. Insects floundered, and where they dragged their wings, left intricate and random trailings in the ash. My own skin felt rough and grainy. It was very hot.

For four days the world remained like that, stripped of movement and poisonous. The air was full of glass. We were advised to stay indoors, and the few who ventured out wore surgical masks or bandanas tied western-style around their faces. Zack was one of them. As the temperatures climbed into the nineties and stayed there, the rest of us sweated it out inside, collecting ash from window ledges, tables, keeping track of particulate counts, and charting wind patterns as assiduously as if they bore another kind of fallout. But not Zack. Zack had a blue kerchief he wore like a bandit and, early each morning and evening, went out to stalk deserted streets in search of poker games. Except the card rooms were all closed and we both knew it. That was his way of making me understand he preferred the aimless wandering and danger to anything we might say in its absence.

II.

ZACK and I had been together seven years, ending up in Missoula when every other place failed. As I always say, "You have to live somewhere." As he always says, "You choose your own landscape." He also says the mountains of Montana are a mad Russian hero standing between him and the thousand-mile steppes. Zack's a gambler and for the longest time I thought he meant he'd take any bet he could get. By the time I figured out it was me or the Russian, we'd painted every room in our apartment clove beige and had begun to count the days between then and when the paper underneath would blister again, the water stains reappear.

Two months passed before the bedroom ceiling erupted into

thousands of tiny bubbles that swelled and split open, peeling back from the dark tan underneath. In another month a brown discoloration was spreading all around the kitchen window. That was in October and I might have made a discreet exit then. But October has always been my favorite month, when everything dies. Besides, Zack had taken up hunting. Where else would I get wild pheasant and duck, never mind that I didn't eat meat? He loved to talk about it while I picked at stir-fried vegetables.

"See this black mark here?" he'd say. "That's where the bullet went in."

I'd add tamari to my rice. He spoke with tenderness of the buck he'd got his first time out, the one whose carcass he had hung in our garage. Even then it was hanging there, stiff but not frozen. You had to wait two weeks at least, he said, to let bacteria get at the meat and start to break it down. Otherwise the kill would be too tough.

What can I say? A woman gets to a certain point. After seven years she drinks more and screws less. And she wants things. I don't know – children, a backyard with fruit trees and a clothesline, some cool basement cupboard where she might store tomatoes and strawberry preserves from her own garden. I'm not saying I'm like that. I'm just saying instincts are instincts, and longings are too. By December our windows were covered with ice and the wind swept down nightly out of the canyons, insinuating itself under all my wool blankets and taking Zack's place at my side.

The first time he stayed out all night I woke up at three and panicked. Sirens pierced the heavy summer darkness. In my bare feet I paced from room to room, wondering whom I should call, what I should do. He'd gone out at seven. I counted eight hours. Then I counted nine. Then I called the Two Horse Café.

"Don't ever call me here again," he said.

"It's four in the morning," I said.

"I know what time it is," he said. "You should be in bed."

A gambler wins and a gambler loses; that's the single sure thing. One way I'd be taken out for dinner and a movie; the other, yelled at for not saving the sports section, not buying beer, not ironing his lucky shirt, not matching his socks. You sleep alone enough, you think about taking a lover. I thought about taking a lover. I took a lover but gave it up almost as soon as it started. I told Zack I wanted to get married.

"You're joking," he said.

"That's not funny," I said.

"I didn't say I thought it was funny. I just said it must be a joke."

Well it wasn't, but it might as well have been. I'd never pretend that wasn't the case. But I wouldn't pretend either that I didn't love him. Don't ask me why. We were so young when we met we had no way of knowing the union we felt so confident of would send us both reeling across greater distances than we could quite imagine then. Later, our faces learned another kind of mobility, suggestive but inscrutable. Riddled with memories, we found it almost impossible to be alone together. Five minutes in the same room with him and my neck knotted, my heart receded. There was nothing I could do to mediate his inaccessibility.

And yet all that came later. In the beginning, in bed on the floor of his bachelor apartment, he taught me how to drink bourbon straight out of the bottle. He nursed me through intestinal disorders in some Mexican village we'd got to on horseback. He told me I would never make a poet, and thank God for that, I took his advice. And he left me so many times those first years that when he finally stopped I was grateful enough for the respite that I did much better than just match his socks: I knitted them, with patterns.

III.

ZACK was playing poker in the back room at the Two Horse not long after rain had finally washed the ash into ridges of silt in the gutters. We had gone into that night charged with something very close to pleasure, but soon our edginess returned, a stale residue of bad Scrabble and too much housebound beer. So I picked a booth away from him and ordered wine instead – white, which came sour and warm. I had my paper, my ink, my fountain pen. I meant to write my sister. First, however, I drank my wine and then ordered more. That's what I liked about bars: you never ran out of whatever it was you were drinking.

"Don't go back to him," my sister always said. "I can't believe you'd really go back to him."

I could appreciate her incredulity, I said, but she had a husband, a career, a future. She said I had my freedom and I went ahead and squandered it. I said for us to talk of something else. With nothing else to say, we said nothing. I went back to him. We corresponded, my sister and I.

Now in the dim light of the bar, between one mural of some miners and nude women and another of Indians on horseback, and in spite of the fact I knew by the sound of Zack's chips he was down, I wrote that our restlessness brings us to cowboys. What I meant for her to understand is that we're not without alternatives, no matter how we feel. I knew she would respond with a blue string tie, telling me to wear it to the local rodeo. Across the room Zack chose another lucky chair and spat tobacco in his coffee cup, and watching him I did not wonder as I might have what, after almost a decade, had finally gone wrong. Everything had gone wrong: we had not had children, he had missed the war, the Russian had gone down on his knees before God. No, that was wrong, I wrote to my sister: *I was the one who went down.* The mountains, after all, did not

seem mad, but ourselves. The way Zack liked to put it I sought
refuge in my fantasies, while he was the opposite, thriving on
risk. I ordered more wine.

All of which is to say that by the time the Indian — I think he
was a Blackfeet — came up to my table, I was feeling both
drunk and introspective. He was squat and swarthy-skinned,
with small, deep-set eyes and clipped black hair, and he was
carrying a fifth of Cabin Still. I filled my pen with ink, pretending not to notice him. He offered me a drink. I told him no. He
sat down anyway and started crying.

"I'm the only one," he said, "the only one. And she blames
me."

"What?" I said.

"Please, ma'am," he said. "Please, you have paper. Please,
I'm too drunk. Please, I'll tell you what to write."

Zack was buying in again. "Write what?"

"A letter. My wife's brother, he just died."

So I let him pick the paper, which I buy by the pound, and
he pointed to a cruel, intense pink. Then he said, "Only this I
understand, only this..." And I wrote *I understand only this*,
"that I loved him like a brother..." *they were brothers* I wrote
down, "and he stabbed me in the back." Later, I understood
that it was a question of family loyalty, that the wife had sided
with the brother, that there were children.

"I want them back," the Indian said, no longer crying.

"Shall I write that?"

He nodded. Zack raked in his first pot. I wrote what the
Indian said. "I want you back," he said. I wrote that too. I
wrote until I had covered a pink sheet, a green sheet, a yellow
sheet, a lavender sheet. I wrote until I had to know.

"How did he die?" I said.

The Indian's eyes narrowed as he straightened his slumped
shoulders and, head reared back, paused with dignity and
menace. Then he drew his finger across his throat. So I read

him what I'd written and he signed with a signature that took up half the page and I sealed and stamped the envelope and gave it back to him. He seemed about to cry again. He kept saying I should drink bourbon.

Later, to my sister, I wrote: *The trouble with alternatives is we don't know what we want.*

Zack was down again when I went back into the night, which was damp and close and smelled faintly of sulfur. Between me and the moon the mountains were grave shadows. I followed the river home. Whatever Zack meant about that Russian, I no longer even thought I knew. I only knew I loved it there and we would never last.

IV.

SINCE girlhood I have dreamed of a man who brings me wild raspberries and roses and chocolates and who knows where to find the hidden places on my body that delight and surprise me as much as they do him. It's a silly dream, a little precious, and I've more or less lost patience with it, but there are moments, odd moments, when it comes back to me.

This was just before the ash or just after it. We were arguing and it was hot. Zack said he'd stopped expecting anything at all of anything, especially me.

"I've given you far too much already," he said. "I've become a Christian for you and if you ask much more, I'll throw you out again."

"A Christian?" I said. "What do you mean, a Christian?"

He looked at me like I was crazy, and because I thought he was I ran into the bedroom and slammed the door. But my nose started to bleed. There was a hot, bleak gush, and a red stain appeared at the knee of my white jeans. "Oh fuck," I said to myself, palm pooling blood just above my chin. "Damn." I turned to take care of myself in the bathroom, but the door was jammed. This had happened before. Zack said you had to push down and pull out. I pushed down and pulled out. Nothing happened.

"Zack," I called.

He didn't answer.

"Goddammit, Zack. The door is stuck."

Still, he didn't answer. Blood was seeping through my fingers and running down my arm to my elbow. I tried the door again. The knob was already smeared and slick.

"My nose, it's bleeding." He said nothing. I screamed, "Zack!"

Some time between then and when the wind changed, sucking the opposite way on that old house and spontaneously loosening the door, Zack went out and my hysteria ceased. Long runnels of blood had thickened on the floor; everywhere the walls were spattered, my jeans, ruined. I felt weak as I cleaned, thinking *Christian, what did he mean — Christian?* Our arguments were like that from the start.

"Since girlhood I have dreamed..." I'd tried to tell Zack the first time we made love.

"I don't want to hear about your fantasies," he said.

When he said nothing else, I said, "What are you thinking about?"

He said, "Don't ever ask me that again."

Six years later I asked him again. He said, "I thought I told you never ask me that."

Were those arguments? I don't know. They were discussions, which quickly turned to arguments because I never knew what he was thinking. He never let me know. And what's the relation between that and my nosebleed? I'd had them before — hiking, during sex — but never in an argument. That was the first induced by an argument. I fell asleep feeling heavy and tainted.

When I woke, Zack was holding my soiled jeans above me.

"What happened here?" he said, sneering. "Did you have an abortion, or what?"

v.

I FOUND myself at one of those literary gatherings common in Missoula — a few macho rancher types with poetic pretensions, a published writer or two, everyone else. Zack was out playing poker. I had left my beaded sweater on the stairs and was trying to make my way through the crush of strangers to the kitchen for beer. Someone offered me whiskey instead. He was short, with a fleshy pug nose, but not otherwise unattractive.

"Do you need a glass?" he said. "Let me get you a glass."

But I didn't need a glass. He smiled. There was loud music on and I knew no one. Only the bottle in my hand felt familiar, so I raised it again and again while he kept on smiling, encouraging my excess. A woman in a black feathered hat came up and put her arms around him.

"Do I know you?" he said. "Do you know her?" he asked me.

"I don't know anyone," I said.

A writer I had heard of took the bottle from me. I dug my empty hands deep into the pockets of my trousers to where the holes let my fingers through to my thighs.

"There's only one understanding I haven't come to yet," the writer said. And then he, too, went away.

The short man had kept the bottle so we kept on talking, exchanging not names but what we did, where we were from, that sort of thing. He was an orphan and had grown up in a boys' home. Once when he was a teenager he'd gotten drunk and driven a stolen car through the window of a television store. Now he was a poet. They were all poets.

I said, "Tell me a poem, one you wrote."

He told me a poem, but by then I was drunk and couldn't concentrate on it very well. People were dancing. He asked me if I wanted to, but I don't dance. We stood there awkwardly. Then he told me he admired a woman who was down to earth and not trying to conform to some kind of Barbie-doll image. When he asked if I was down to earth, I told him I lived with a gambler.

"You can't get much more down to earth than that," I said. He said, "Zack?"

I said nothing, so he put his arms around me. The aged silk of my blouse ripped down the front. He touched my breast. We kissed for a long time. There weren't so many people dancing anymore. The bottle was lower than I believed was necessary, or even possible.

Later, we went out into a warm, dawn rain. At the corner he asked me again to go home with him.

"You can forget about Zack," I said. He kissed me. "But I'm not coming either."

There was a scene. Then he left me at the corner. It was a mile back to our apartment, but I walked past where he lived anyway, wanting to go up. I also walked past the Two Horse, where Zack was still playing, but had no desire to go in there. By the time I got home the sun was bright behind the mountains. My blouse, which I had sewn of fabric from the attic in my parents' house – my grandmother's, I supposed – was torn to ribbons. I had lost my sweater. Still, I felt neither regret nor longing when I stuffed the blouse in the trash under orange rinds and yoghurt containers. I felt exactly the same way half an hour later as I fell into a numbing, dreamless sleep.

VI.

IT'S LIKE that town fanatic who had visions of the end of the world. We'd find his announcements nailed to our door. Sometimes he projected specific dates and hours; others, he left maps to civil defense shelters. There were lists of what to bring – how much water, candy bars, a deck of cards – and instructions for making your home cellar safe. Finally, he littered the floors of his own home with stones, timber, and mud, and went underground one afternoon at five o'clock. We never heard from him again.

Think of our lives as you would, say, rocks in a path. You've climbed some, you've come to a meadow, the trail disappears in boggy ground. So you wander around for awhile until you find it again on the other side, and there are some rocks – small white ones, large black ones, it doesn't really matter. What matters is that more than anything you want to believe they were placed and arranged there for some divine purpose, but you know in your heart it's only random.

As each of the designated doomsday hours passed, we touched ourselves and found we were alive. It was that easy, and that difficult. Not that we didn't want to be alive, but that we wanted to be different. And we weren't. Look, I know it's possible to reconceive events, change whole lives, even history, with a simple distortion of memory. At least I think it's possible. I've heard it explained and it makes sense in my own head. The only problem is with Zack and me you're dealing with a fundamental resistance to looking at anything except in its clearest, coldest context. There's that. And I guess there is also that this is my context.

So if I say that the morning before the ash came, I let Zack make love to me, maybe I did and maybe I didn't. And if I say that later we went shopping and argued over scented toilet paper, again, maybe so, maybe not. I did push the cart ahead of him. He did trail behind, muttering insults. On the way home we took the back road, the one that skirts the canyons. I pretended it was a pleasure drive and remarked on how many people were out playing Frisbee, pushing infants in blue strollers. I thought if I watched a ball game on TV with Zack, he might take me out too. I thought we might walk up the river. Instead there was another ball game and the first beer of the afternoon. Zack only noticed me once the whole time. I don't know what beer it was, but it must have been a station break. It must have been eating at him too, what he wanted to tell me, his instruction.

He got up and went to the window. He said, "Come here." I did. He pointed to the hills and said, "You'll never see them this green again. It's the season, the rains. This is as green as they'll ever get."

VII.

WE HIKED up out of the heat of the valley, determined to leave behind the noise of the city and our quarreling. But we had gotten a late start and the thirty-mile dirt road to the trail head took more time than we had planned. Zack struck a steady, rapid pace and, longer-strided than I, drew quickly ahead. I tightened the hip strap on my pack, hoisted it higher, and, forcing myself to increase my own speed, studied the beat of my red tennis shoes.

The trail climbed steeply for three miles, moving in and out of forest, before leveling off to follow a long, shallow lake, edged with the algae of late summer. A short, almost vertical rise at the end of that lake led to another plunged deep in the hollow where five mountains met. Zack was sitting on a log that sliced straight toward the blue center of water. If he heard me behind him he made no sign and, except for the occasional sideways movement of his head to spit out tobacco, remained motionless. I was hungry so I ate some cheese. He filled the water bottle and we went on.

We hiked another nine miles that afternoon, crossing one ridge and arriving at a third lake just at nightfall. Birds, which had cried out at our intrusion all through dusk, were suddenly silent. Wind brushed the surface of the water once, soughed up through the trees, and was still. By moonlight, perched on a boulder, I saw that this lake, much smaller than the other two, was almost perfectly round. We had found the only beach.

For three days we camped there, hiking off after breakfast over ridges, down creeks to other lakes where I swam and Zack crouched in the sun. We were as anxious to wear ourselves out as we were to exchange each view we achieved for the next. From meadows we could survey peaks above; from those same peaks, the sweep of mountain ranges to the plains. There, exhaustion precluded the necessity of speech. And by night we were content to warm our hands at the fire and point out constellations without thought of their significance. We made kind but not passionate love and slept well.

Then, on the third night, a late summer storm blew in. Wind stirred a new desire in me Zack didn't share. All night I lay awake beside him, listening to owls. What I felt, I think, was not dread but an inconsolable loss. By dawn I knew our time was up.

All my muscles ached as we broke camp, and I discovered several blisters on my toes and one large one on the pad of my foot. Zack was in such a hurry I fumbled everything. We started back toward the car in a mood of resignation.

It was like that the whole way. The rain kept up, off and on, until we were soaked through and chilled. If I stopped to rest, Zack worried we'd be late getting back; if I taped my feet, he complained I was using all the Band-Aids. When I paused to wash my face in a creek, he badgered me from the other side. The closer we got to the end of the trail, the more in a hurry he seemed, as if having made the first move toward departure, he wanted nothing more than to complete it.

In the end I gave up and let him get ahead of me – I don't

know, maybe fifteen minutes, maybe half an hour. I was aware only of my physical pain as I passed that first lake and started on the remaining three miles toward the car, where what had begun as escape and become ordeal would finally be over. For myself, almost, what I was returning to seemed preferable to what I was enduring at the moment.

After what felt like an impossible distance, the trail widened, turning into a road, and then the trees broke enough so that I could see the metallic blue of the car glistening ahead. I unstrapped my pack and hurried toward it, but just at that moment Zack started coming at me with a black piece of hose raised in his fist — as if to say, before I even knew that porcupines had eaten all our gas lines and sucked out all our gas, that I had done it, I was responsible. We were alone in that part of that country with a thirty-mile dirt road between us and a deserted western highway. It might have been funny, but it wasn't.

VIII.

OUR LAST October we found the tracks of what looked to be a wounded deer. The snow was dry and soft and would not hold the shape of the hoof, but the trail of blood was clear. We followed it for several miles before coming to the top of a ridge from which we could trace the brutal red smear all the way down one slope and up a neighboring wash. By the quantities of blood that had been spilled, it seemed the animal must be enormous. The day was brittle with cold. For the third time since we started, a snow flurry threatened overhead, but then passed by without disturbing a stillness as utter as the one the ash had brought. Overwhelmed by the magnitude of our isolation, I bent my head to the frozen earth to listen for some other sign of life. I imagined the hunter in gray morning light: *As he raises the familiar weight of the gun, he thinks of the buck as a gift from heaven. It is not possible for him to miss this shot. Like two gods they observe each other, the hunter and the hunted. Each is half-crazed with the nearness of his antagonist. In the instant before he fires, the man is suffused by a rush of tenderness for the animal that embraces the entire universe and interrupts the necessity for precision.*

The Meaning of
Their Names

CONSTANCE had visions of nuclear holocaust. She'd had them all her life, really, ever since the Rosenbergs were killed and her mother said to her father, "Now thanks to them we could be burned alive." Constance, who was four then, had a dream in which the father ate his peas and no matter where she ran — into the closet, under the bed, up the stairs — it turned into a fireplace. The stairs just disappeared and she fell beneath the flames, trying to run as she sank into deep beds of coals. But now that Constance was grown up, she knew that when the time came there'd be no time for running, and so she was doing her running beforehand — not away from but toward the danger zone, which she meant in her own way to defuse.

It was June and at five in the morning the Sacramento Greyhound bus depot was as crowded as it had been half the night before when Constance finished scrubbing out the ladies' room and went home to pack her personal belongings in the purple shopping bag she'd got free at Macy's, though she bought all her clothes at Woolworth's. Today for her trip she had chosen the thin blue flowered dress with pearl buttons, and the white sweater, and her lightest of pale blue slippers. Constance's eyes were blue too, also perpetually startled, but her face had a rare, reliable quality, just short of grave, that saved it. As she waited she hummed, she shifted her bag, she pressed against the polished glass of Gate 4 – destinations, Salt Lake City, Cheyenne, Washington, D.C. Already behind her the floor was streaked with boot and suitcase markings, and there were cigarette butts and candy and Dorito wrappers, and over in the corner, a soiled paper diaper. But what did all that matter now when Constance had her bus pass pinned to the inside of her cool cotton slip, her packed purple shopping bag, and her manila envelope thick with petitions for nuclear disarmament?

Still, if Constance had her purpose, she also had her memories, her sense of the familiar, what she valued more than anything but peace. Half her life this year she'd lived in Sacramento, the better part by far, during which she'd learned to find the freshest quart of milk, the cheapest grilled cheese sandwich, the reddest pair of go-aheads. In the Greyhound coffee shop the waitresses would serve her just half a cup of coffee, to keep it hot, without her asking. The man who put newspapers in the boxes left one for her at the ticket counter free. She was liked and she liked it, but a first strike was a first strike nonetheless, and Sacramento was a target.

In the same way, all those years before, between the day the Rosenbergs were killed and the Cuban missile crisis, Constance had been terrified of her mother. The woman had a way about her, maybe calculated, maybe not, as if her own personal terror, somehow transformed to spite, might alone be enough to call down the wrath of nations. If her mother said *Now the Russians will orbit a man in space,* the Russians orbited a man in space; if her mother said *Now the Chinese will get the Bomb,* the Chinese got the Bomb. Constance calculated lifespans, particularly hers, in terms of projected technological developments:

how long before how many had the knowledge and capacity to blow the world up. Then the Cuban missile crisis changed her whole perspective: survival taught Constance the power of firmness. To her mother she said she preferred to be called Constance. "Connie you've been called since the day you were born," her mother said. "Connie you'll be called until you die." Constance bridled but kept the peace, until to keep it further she had to pack and leave. It hadn't been easy then and it wouldn't be easy now, but no one had called Constance *Connie* since.

THE DRIVER, when he started taking tickets, nodded to Constance and did not check her pass. Constance took the seat behind his, propped her feet up on her bag, folded her red hands neatly in her lap, and watched the other passengers as they boarded, watching her. Her gaze was ingenuous, inviting, theirs guarded, for Constance was a small woman, boyish, hard, and muscular, and with enormous blond braids coiled and coiled around her tiny head and the daintiest, whitest teeth. Pearls, Duane had called them, perfect shining pearls all in a perfect shining row. Constance closed her lips, still smiling. A girl in a tight Budweiser T-shirt and green heels tripped as she got on. Constance smiled harder. The girl caught her balance, hurrying back. An older man, potbellied, slow, with a black cane and white cowboy hat, tipped his hat kindly but also moved back. The women with babies, the fat boys with books, they all had their preferred locations on the bus, and not any beside Constance, who still kept on watching them with that startled expression she had no control over, for Constance had it planned out in her head.

At first she and her seatmate would talk about what people talk about, probably the other person's family or health or religious beliefs, or maybe just the weather, where they were going, things like that, it didn't matter. Because time would, as it does, go on and they would cross the valley, there would be foothills, and then the long climb into the mountains. Constance smiled, more to herself. There, when they got to the mountains, it would be so green and cool, with a carpet of needles and small yellow flowers, and though you wouldn't be able to smell it on the bus, that fresh pine scent, like the more expensive brands of disinfectant. Constance, who had never been to the mountains, had seen pictures and knew. A feeling of peace would come over the travelers. They'd smile across the aisle, introduce themselves, and offer to share sandwiches or hold their neighbor's child, just the same as in Constance's dream when she defused the last bomb in the world and there was a great party in a meadow full of flowers, and people dancing to the music of fiddles and flutes, and children trailing bright-colored balloons.

Yes that would be the perfect time, up in the mountains, to bring out her petitions and give one first to the person beside her, then to the front, to the back, to the other side. Maybe the driver would announce it, maybe he'd let her talk on his little microphone. And what she would say then, she would say about nuclear war – its pros and cons – in such a way that no one would refuse to sign, if anyone ever could. Already to herself she was counting up the signatures, one for every person on the bus. And if you multiplied that number by the number possible on each petition, and if each person took only one petition with that person to that person's destination for people there to sign...

The bus pulled suddenly down familiar streets and Constance caught her breath. There was the rosebush, heavy and red, which not three months before she'd worried frost might kill; there, the Orange Julius where sometimes she had orange juice. They turned left, they turned right, Constance pressed her forehead to the window. Behind this fence that spring she'd found a pond with lilies and a waterfall, three swans, and fist-sized goldfish. It was a sweet early April dusk when she had wandered past, and heard the swans sing out in mating, and stopped to part the vines. Week after week she had returned, listening for the squawk of ducklings. Now she closed her eyes and turned the pond into a fireplace, flames spouting up where water pummeled down.

LEAVING a place was not at all like arriving, the way sixteen years before Constance had arrived in Sacramento with nothing but her handbag and the memory of her mother stationed in front of the family TV. "They should send them all to jail," her mother kept insisting. "Communists, nigger-lovers, Berkeley free-speech jerks. What's this country coming to?" Constance didn't care so much about the country then. She cared that her mother would be turning on her next: "Your hair's a mess. You have no breasts. And why, oh why do you stay home Friday nights?" Constance left on Friday night and arrived in Sacramento in the morning, so of course when Duane smiled and offered her work she thought it would be fine to sweep out the litter and scour the restrooms: it was a job, and she liked things to be clean.

She liked things as they turned out, all in all. She took a small apartment near the depot; she took to a routine of working days, wandering evenings; it was fine. Sacramento was fine. The mall had concrete fountains to cool her feet in during summer; Breuner's had animated windows at Christmas. Breuner's was nice, really, any time of year. Constance liked to go there and dream of matching bedroom sets, if only she could think what to do with all the drawers. Put things in them probably – string and picture postcards and her pay stubs and all those flowers she collected from the edges of gardens.

But then that was the way she had always been, Constance, delighted with small pleasures and with her strong likes and dislikes, so much more pronounced than those of others, and also lacking any sense of irony, humor, or proportion. Even as a girl she'd lacked the grace of compromise, become excited over trifles – red shoelaces, snow – and been as likely to feel distressed if chunks of white came off with the shell of her hardboiled egg as she was when the President was killed. She also read books backward from her very first primer, a notion which her mother hoped would pass, but it didn't. Constance's notions never passed, and the way she had of framing them kept her apart from all other children, except for a short time a girl named Jan.

Jan moved to town the February of Constance's eleventh year and from the back seat in the last row stared across the classroom, her green eyes clear and knowing, at Constance. Constance stared back. The teacher took her aside and explained, "Jan's back is curved like an 'S.' " "Snake," Jan told Constance, who thought the other girl's red braids and queer slumped shoulders beautiful. So they started sharing ribbons, Jan and Constance, for their hair, and lunches out among the boulders at the far end of the playground. Behind them, round California hills humped into bleak sky; chipmunks scolded; wind tore at live oak, buckbush, manzanita. Constance particularly liked the wind, which made her feel alive and intimate. She'd never felt that way before, with the craziest ideas and not at all timid. Once she asked Jan what she thought it would be like. "*I* think," Constance said, "there will be a hot blow to the forehead, and then..." Jan broke apart an Oreo and licked at the sugary icing. "If it comes to that," she said, "I'd just as soon be dead."

ON THE bus the seats weren't as comfortable as Constance had remembered from her other bus trip years before. Her feet didn't touch the floor and her head, which hit right in the center of the rest hump, was angled forward at an awkward tilt. After the first thirty miles her neck began to ache. She tried to shift without seeming to squirm; she sat straight upright and pretended she was watching a Greyhound pay TV. It really was like that, with the green-tinted window for the screen and all the cars outside and the riders in them, and every half hour or so, another town, another station, except naturally there wasn't any music or talking, and no real characters either. Things could get boring without music or characters, so Constance hummed and made up stories about all the people she saw and how they were almost killed in the nuclear holocaust but then by God's grace at the last terrible minute war was averted and everyone was saved. Constance especially liked saving little babies and every truck driver who reminded her of Duane.

THE TRUE thing is, from the time Duane hired her to the time he noticed her playing "Let's Make a Deal" for a matching bedroom set during her only morning break, Constance thought about his smile which showed, beneath a waxed red mustache, two front teeth shifted one tooth over to the left. It was the strangest thing. She'd be sweeping out the lobby and see him talking to a ticket agent, and the way he was leaning over the other girl would make her feel something where she never had before, almost like bomb drills at school, but nice. Or he'd come up behind her and put his hand on her shoulder, and all her blood would rush down. Constance never knew what to say at those times. Even later at home she'd feel unnerved. "Duane winked at me today," she'd say. "Did I wink back? Why didn't I wink back?" Then she'd take her chicken pot pie from the oven and as she waited for it to cool, uncoil and unbraid her hair and sometimes unbutton her blouse just one more button. "Do you think he'd like me better this way?" she'd say. But by morning, every morning, she'd have lost her nerve again and gone to work as neat and tidy as she'd always been before.

Only feelings are feelings, especially certain kinds, and so it was inevitable that Duane would come to her that day she was trying for a matching bedroom set and take her to the baggage room and lead her to a box back in the far corner with Oriental writing on it and a two-week-old received date, and then ask her what she thought the sounds were that were coming from it. Constance bent over the box and listened. Duane was standing behind her. The sounds were not quite peeps, not quite chirps, a little squawkish. Constance said, "I think it's ducks." Duane put his hand on her shoulder. Constance said, "Sometimes on Sunday I go to the park and feed the ducks stale bread. This sounds like baby ducks." Duane's hand moved. She started to undo the string. He started to undo her hair. It was cool in the baggage room, with the smell of leather and of Duane's cheap cologne. There were so many ducks inside the box, little yellow fluffs, Constance couldn't count them all. Instead, she found herself counting the fingers on Duane's hands which had come around at last and were reaching for her buttons, down her front. Soon she wasn't counting anything at all.

IN THE mountains nothing happened, and in Reno nothing happened either except that Constance won five slot machine nickels and bought Wrigley's chewing gum to share with the person she sat with, as she was done waiting for someone to sit with her. Even so it was hard to decide. Again and again Constance wandered up the aisle, down the aisle, finally selecting a broad-shouldered woman in a green skirt and sweater with a small TV on her lap.

"Ma'am?" Constance said. "Please, ma'am, do you want a piece of gum?"

The woman looked up, smiling, and extended her hand. "I'm Lucette, from Montreal."

"Constance," Constance said, "on my way to Washington."

Lucette made a sound in her throat like "ahh." Constance sat down. A black man brushed her knee, heading toward the rear, and a girl in Levis stretched out across both seats opposite. Lucette made that sound again. Shy suddenly, Constance checked her envelope, crammed in the top of her purple shopping bag. Then a man in a navy undershirt and shiny black polyester slacks paused before them, staring down from above. A tic at the corner of his nose made his whole face jump and he smelled of cheap aftershave and whiskey. Lucette nudged Constance.

"*That* kind of man," she said. "*That's* the kind of man you have to watch."

"Watch what?" Constance said.

"They beat their wives. They slap their children to sleep," Lucette said, fiddling with the knobs of her TV.

For one hundred miles across the desert, Lucette watched a ball game while Constance tried to match the teams up with dark uniforms and light uniforms. Every once in awhile the man put his head over the back of her seat and, grinning, asked the score. Underneath his chin, along the contour of his jaw, a red and black tattoo twisted like a diamond-backed snake. When he talked, the snake moved. Constance wanted to make the snake be still, but her head was full of her mission of peace and all she could think about was how did a person begin: with everything turning into a fireplace, or with the hot blow to the forehead? Lucette had such a stern forehead, high and so indelicately lined Constance had to fight back an impulse to reach over and smooth it out. What she would have given to fill this other woman and the man and the rest of them with peace! But without the right and true convincing words she could only wait for the ball game to be over. It was a very long ball game. It would go on forever. And then midway through the sixth inning the TV reception went out.

"Oh," Constance said. "Oh."

Lucette laughed. "What the hell. My team was losing."

The man's head appeared above them, the snake's tail wiggling excitedly, but Lucette said something that made it disappear again. Constance was nervously prying at the flap of her envelope, which had stuck with moisture. Lucette stowed the TV under the seat.

"Men," she muttered, "they're all the same. What's he been drinking, I wonder? What's that you have there?" she asked Constance, sitting up.

Constance got the envelope open and thrust a petition at her. Then there was a pause, longer than she had anticipated. In her head she kept formulating arguments: *The birds will be blinded, water will burn, our children will not be like us.*

"I'll sign," the man behind them said. "Just give me a pen. Sign what?"

Constance said nothing.

At last Lucette said, "Tell me about it. I'm a nurse. *I* volunteered for Vietnam."

"Didn't I say I'd sign?" the man said.

But Constance didn't hear him now, heard nothing but the sudden beating of her own heart. She couldn't breathe and there were colored specks at the edges of her vision. Lucette was saying it was time, past time. Constance was trying to count but had forgotten her numbers. What came after seven? It wasn't possible. Lucette had been *there*, at the other war. And since she had been there, she might have, could she have...

"Oh sure," Lucette said when Constance got her question out, "I knew hundreds of Duanes. Duane this, Duane that..."

Constance grabbed her arm. "No please, I have to know. Did this Duane have red hair — red hair and crooked teeth?"

"I knew a redheaded Duane," the man behind them said, then got up and went to the back for a smoke. Lucette looked away too, but not quickly enough that Constance didn't see the new look come into her eyes, with something sad about it, and tender, and made almost unbearable by what must have been an inconsolable loss. Constance waited, maybe one minute, maybe ten, she'd lost all sense of time. At last Lucette said that, well yes, he'd had red hair, he'd had blond hair, he'd had black hair. They'd all of them had hair if it wasn't burned off.

THE BABY ducks were all over the floor before Duane and Constance remembered them, and Constance ran around naked, laughing and scooping them up to lay in the cradle of Duane's cupped hands. They filled their pockets and kissed some more. Constance took home seven ducklings she made a place for in her bathtub and kept them there until one died. It was very sad. All one night she knelt on the cold tile floor, watching it in hopes it might get up, but the feathers were so damp and already there was a bad smell. Afterwards, because Duane said it was best, she let him put the others out of their misery. That was the only time he came to her apartment, and he was so cool and calculated sitting on the porcelain edge of her tub and snapping, one by one between his fingers, the six remaining yellow necks. Constance cried and wished she'd thought to set them free in the park, but when Duane found out what was wrong, he said they weren't natural ducks anyway and would have died soon enough in that kind of wild environment. Constance felt something funny twist inside her when she heard the words *that kind of wild environment*, and she never could, no matter what, forget them.

But for three years, as long as Constance was with Duane, Constance didn't care, for though the way they were together was not like other people, neither was Constance, and so she was happy. Nothing could have pleased her more than that she and Duane meet as they did in the baggage room for one thing and one thing only, the way they both preferred, simple, to the point and beyond the necessity of either thought or speech. She liked the musty smells too, and the dim light, and the cold hard feel of the luggage rack beneath her. Far away she could hear the people in the station; close, Duane's breathing and his heart. That was best. That, and that they'd dress when they were done and go their separate ways, knowing they'd be at it again before too long. That really was best — mute acquiescence, perfect agreement — for if the nature of solitude were deathly still and luminescent as a nimbus, Duane had let himself so cleanly into Constance's it was altered only insofar as it was made safe. Nothing, not even nuclear war, could destroy this, what she had with Duane. How could there be nuclear war when there was this?

LUCETTE'S hand was on Constance's shoulder, not shaking or squeezing but just resting there, more an acknowledgment than an apology. They sat like that for awhile, the two women, one large, one small, before either could find it in herself to break the silence. Then it was Lucette who spoke, not at all shy to admit she dreamed of peace too. She gestured up and down the aisle with a broad, expansive sweep of her arm.

"We all do," she said, "every one of us on this bus. How could we not?"

But Constance was still upset. She frowned. She didn't know. "If all people dream of peace," she said, "why are things the way they are?"

"Ah that," Lucette said. "That's just the way it is. Why does that man have a snake beneath his chin?"

Constance frowned harder. The man seemed fine to her. She really was trying to understand.

"Well never mind then," Lucette said. "I may be right, but I may be wrong. Let's ask the others and see what they say."

And by the time they reached Chicago, where their routes diverged, she and Constance had done just that, discovering in so doing what Lucette had said was true. For everyone along the way – including all the drivers and the girl in green heels and her new boyfriend and, before he got thrown out in Iowa for drunkenness, the tattooed man, who as he was leaving told Constance she had such pretty eyes and too good a heart for this world – had signed, and Constance had her hope and optimism back.

But it was somehow changed. She didn't know. Either people signed right off, or they signed after thinking about it. In the end their motives were the same – for their own good. Constance wanted that their motives should be different. She wanted that they shouldn't have their weaknesses and prejudices, which showed so clearly in their eyes, in how they slung their bodies back against their seats. Where had they been when the other war was on? Why had they strayed so far from home? Constance, who knew about fear, couldn't hold theirs against them. But Constance had seen beyond her own fear and believed if they did too everything might suddenly be changed.

Only Constance was a small person, just like them, and such grace was not in her power. Grace of that magnitude lay alone in the power of the greater men and women to whom she would deliver her petitions. So she knew in her heart all she could tell the others, if she could tell them anything, was simply to go home, keep tidy kitchens and the peace, and let themselves be heard. However small they might be, they might, by living just and proper lives, transcend the limitations of their size and move the greater people to recognize the meaning of their names. Constance kept counting names. To her they appeared as the multitudes.

IT WASN'T nuclear war but the war in Vietnam Constance should have feared for herself years back, for when it reached a certain pitch, Duane enlisted. Nine months later he was dead. And what Constance felt then was not grief so much as betrayal, for there had been about their wanton encounters something that, while they were taking place, eased an unacknowledged emptiness inside her, and while they weren't, exacerbated it. But Constance had cared so little for introspection and the common realms of meaning in those days the terms seemed unimportant. All that seemed important was that she should be in the baggage room at the designated times. *That* had been her mistake, her only mistake, apparently small but in fact of such proportions it took Duane's untimely death to teach her what she'd really felt was love. Not even Constance's mother could have argued with that, but it changed everything. For in Constance's head now Duane took the only form she could imagine for him – husband. He had been husband and she had been wife.

Constance didn't know what to do with that, so at first she did what she'd always done – go to work, wander, dream of matching bedroom sets, feed ducks. But there were different laws in operation now, and little by little Duane's world intruded. Constance tried thinking about it. She thought and thought. Eventually she thought to ask the man who put newspapers in the boxes for a copy and read it back to front, intensely interested, as she was when she was young, to get to the beginning and see how it all started. And then she thought since Duane was killed in Vietnam she should demonstrate against the war, but Constance was terrified of crowds and rhetoric. She thought about writing the President, but what could she possibly say? At last she thought if she could somehow memorialize Duane's passing it would be as if he never passed at all. Order would be restored and Constance could return to the steadiness of purpose in her own life her perfect isolation had always in the past sustained for her.

So Constance started keeping casualty figures on blue and yellow note cards – blue for Americans, yellow for Vietnamese.

The figures increased alarmingly. Constance bought more cards, and then more cards and more cards. It was frightening. She filled recipe files, shoe boxes, and every empty drawer in her imaginary matching bedroom set. The war ended, but she couldn't stop. She bought fat black felt pens and started keeping records on the walls of her apartment. Names lost significance. She resorted to numbers: 7,000 in Argentina; 45,000 in El Salvador; 80,000 in Lebanon; 2,000,000 in Cambodia. Constance thought about the number two million; she thought about the murder in the bus depot that fall. And she kept adding and adding: 2,000 in Northern Ireland; 5,000 in Turkey; 10,000 in Chile; 25,000 in Zimbabwe, in Ethiopia, in Guatemala; 50,000 in Nicaragua; 100,000 in Afghanistan; 2,000,000 in Nigeria. The deaths went on and on, ten million in all, so engaging Constance in the minutiae of recording and remembering that she forgot for almost a decade the other, greater danger. But that was not to be escaped and Constance knew it, and so with the resumption of the Cold War in the eighties she was not taken by surprise but rather, at last, inspired to action. For that kind of number was unimaginable. That kind of number was not to be written or fathomed. That kind of number sent her reeling, eventually off to Washington, D.C., armed with her petitions and faith.

But washington, when she arrived, was not what she expected. It was hot and crowded and noisy, and though so much was the same – the black plastic waiting chairs and gates with destinations and people traveling places – not at all like Sacramento, which Constance suddenly felt very far from. There, she had the confidence of habit; here, she felt crumpled and confused. Her ankles were swollen, her neck wouldn't turn without pain, and all over she had an unclean feeling. Just if Constance could get clean, that would help, and maybe spend a moment to compose herself. Only where was the baggage room in Washington, where the clean and private washroom?

Constance stared disconsolately at her bag and envelope. No one cared very much about cleanliness in Washington. The lobby smelled of rancid hot dogs and if a Coke spilled on the floor, the Coke stayed there, with people tracking Coke footprints all over and the sticky slap-hiss of their shoes peeling off. They had so many different colored shoes, this huge, dark, steaming throng, darker than in Sacramento, black not brown, and much more crushed together. Bodies had no discreteness. Arms were as likely to wrap themselves around you as to shove you out of the path, faces to spit as to nuzzle at your neck, hips to knock you down as to rub you there. It was all one thing, flesh against flesh. Constance stumbled, grabbing for her envelope as her bag spilled out in front. The voice on the loudspeaker repeated you should watch your personal belongings. Constance watched hers scatter. If only, if only she could just sit down.

Constance didn't know how long it took, but somehow she made it to the far wall near the occupied TV's where she found herself towering above a no-legged beggar on his platform. Instinctively she tried to give him a petition, but he cursed and pushed himself away without knowing what it was. Near tears, Constance hugged the envelope. She missed Lucette. She even missed the man with the snake beneath his chin. What kind of snake was it really, she wondered. A rattlesnake? A cobra? She shuddered. Someone was watching her, she could feel it. Then she saw him and was washed through with relief.

Not twenty feet away a nice-looking young man in a uniform was watching her with interest, and his TV wasn't on. Constance smiled, hoping he might offer her his seat. He didn't move, but his socks were so white and his blond hair cropped so close to his head and his cheeks so smooth and pink and covered with such soft down Constance wanted to touch it. She wanted suddenly to sit down in his lap and rest her head upon his shoulder. The last time she'd seen Duane he'd been wearing the same uniform. It was a fine uniform, khaki and neat. Constance smiled again, this time meeting his eyes. Then they couldn't look away. Beneath his white eyelashes green irises, flecked with gold, pulsed, making the dark pupils big, small. Constance's own eyes grew wider. They kept staring and staring at each other, until after awhile the boy – for he was really more that than a man – said something to a squat, black woman at his side, who shook her head and left. And Constance took her place.

So much she wanted to talk to the boy, to thank him, to tell him what she'd been through and why and ask his help, but she was so tired and the chair was so comfortable – familiar and curved just right for her body – that almost at once she started drifting off to sleep. The sounds of the station were reduced to a hum. Colors merged. Beside her she could feel the boy's eyes caress her, from her big blond braids to her pale blue slippers.

And then in that state, half awake, half asleep, terrifyingly, Constance heard the bells of game shows the way she heard the school bell long ago one February noon with Jan – three loud short rings, a pause; three loud short rings, another pause. Constance knew at that moment what her mother said was true, and she bent and put her arm across her forehead to shield it from the hot blow, calling helplessly out that they must go in, they must go in: *This could be a real war.* The young man at her side shifted nervously. But Jan was already hiding deep among scrub oak, laughing and calling back that she'd rather be dead, she'd rather be dead, she'd rather...

"I wasn't constant," Constance said. "We could have been burned alive, but she was my friend and I wasn't constant."

"Ma'am?" the young man said.

And that's what Constance had said years before, after, when they were safe, to the teacher, in front of everyone: *We could have been burned alive and Jan wasn't even scared. She's with them. She wasn't even scared.* The game show bells went right on ringing. In spite of herself Constance laughed out loud, but not like it was funny, for now she knew that's what Duane had meant.

"*That's* what he meant," she said.

"Ma'am?" the young man said again, and in his voice there was a queer edge too. "Who, ma'am?"

But Constance was thinking that a person was born to a certain world and that outside that world, in the wild environment, anything could happen. So yes it was Constance herself who had been Jan's wild environment, and Jan's back had curved and curved, and then Jan moved away. And Vietnam was Duane's, and Duane was dead. And Washington... Constance sat upright, awake at last, and looked around her. Maybe *this* was *her* wild environment. She had come so far with such great hopes, gathering the multitudes within her. But now they were without again, surrounding, closing in.

"Ma'am?" the young man said for the third time, and finally the odd voice broke through so that when Constance turned to him everything cleared. Once more she felt filled with love, for in his bland, almost featureless face she saw them all, Lucette and Jan and Duane and the man with the snake chin and the drivers and the rest. Constance had never known such serenity as this. Between them, her and the boy, whom she loved, they contained the multitudes. The boy stood. Constance did too, smiling, loving him so. Maybe all wouldn't go as smoothly as she'd planned. Maybe her petitions would have to wait until she found the right, the proper time and place to deliver them. But it would be all right. She could work for awhile here at the D.C. Greyhound station, scrubbing down, disinfecting. And as she did, she could collect more signatures, and more and more, starting now with the young man standing straight and tall before her.

Constance reached into her envelope. They boy took a step back. Constance grabbed his arm. The boy was shaking his head but she wasn't looking at him. She was looking at the multitudes. To the multitudes she thrust a blank petition. The boy put up his hand. Constance opened her mouth to sing out then and there with the message of the multitudes, but just as her voice caught hold of the first, most important word — *peace* — it choked it back again. For when the boy saw what she wanted, he didn't sign. He turned away.

Burning the Lost Country

I.

N ORM'S purpose came to him the way
God did – one raw March day on the eastern bank of the lower
Bitterroot five miles out of Missoula. The two events were not
concurrent, and the former preceded the latter by almost three
years. Though both were inevitable, the order could not have
been reversed. Visions, Norm knows now, are like Lea's
glazes – the one determined by the other, holy or unholy, each
unspeakably blessed. For to sin is to enter into ultimate salvation. For to render oneself up to righteousness, one way or
another, is to see clearly what one never saw before.

It was March, as I say, and Norm had walked up the river
because his house was small and cold and because Lea had not
answered his letters. For two months he had written every
week, determinedly, on Thursdays. He stayed sober to write
the letters, that was part of his bargain with himself. And he
wrote as eloquently as he could about how everything he'd
said was true, only worse. The hills, since his brief absence,
were harder to recognize than ever. Anaconda Copper folded;
the town of Anaconda died. Displaced men passed through
Missoula and though Norm wanted to embrace them, to tell

them *you* stay, there was no place left for them there either: *They had been usurped.* What was it Lea had said? "A state is just a state. Look at California." Norm looked at California and passed beyond grief to despair. So he went home, but Lea wouldn't follow. So he wrote, but she wouldn't answer. So he walked up the river that raw March day to escape the crush of town and the angry whine of chain saws and the barefoot Weaver's Guild, and came instead to a spot where it curved with such serenity and grace that he stopped, rooted just there for no other reason than that he knew he had come to the end of even all that.

If Norm looked hard enough he could see places on the trees where in a month or two there would be buds. It had been warm for the season and here and there along the path snow had melted off completely, showing patches of rich dark earth. Somewhere in the distance an angry bird screamed, probably a jay. At Norm's feet a sluggish salamander curled, freezing when Norm knelt to it and stroked its sleek, still belly. Had he been Lea and the salamander clay, he would have crushed it then. But he didn't. He just turned back all at once and walked five miles into town straight to the Lorenz Hotel Saloon. For from the belly of the salamander the haze of indirection that had for two months now plagued Norm was lifted. For Lea also said, not once but many times, "So prove it if you can, Norm. Prove every lie you've ever told."

II.

N orm and Lea met at a demonstration against the Rancho Seco nuclear plant in Sacramento, twin to Three Mile Island but tidier and with a better reputation, as a consequence of which the demonstration was small, not violent, unheard of. A handful of people went out to stare grimly at the towers, that was all. And no, I can't tell you what became of the others.

Maybe one later scaled the fence at San Diablo. Maybe one went home and, inspired, left her husband. They were a civilized crew for the most part, middle class and terrified not so much for their children, as they said, but for themselves.

Norm, however, was different, a broad-backed, stern-faced law student from Montana; and so was Lea, a whimsical potter who dabbed scented oils behind her ears and polished her nails lavender, green. Norm's sense of smell was so strong that years before he had found hippies on his father's land just by sniffing out the marijuana, like a dog. He could also, hunting deer, almost always smell them first. Thus, at Rancho Seco, despite the thick dust and heavy sweetness of lupine, Norm was aware of Lea's spice somewhere in the ineffectual crowd and sought it out. She was barely five feet tall and intent on the towers. Norm stood behind her, savoring the scent, half again as large as she. And as with women he has always been shy he would have been content with that, gone home to study property and torts, if Lea hadn't turned to him and said, "They're so beautiful and evil, don't you think?"

She took him back to the garage that served as both her studio and home, and without saying anything else took him to her, lifting her thin white legs high around him and stroking the backs of his thighs with her feet in such a way as to arouse in Norm the kind of longing no act of sex can ever assuage. Afterwards Lea chopped up vegetables and sautéed them with curry. She only had chopsticks to eat with. Her nails, dark green, as she handled hers, caught the light from so many candles, reproachfully glinting at Norm from the other side of the low round table, who found though he wanted to leave now he couldn't.

And of course he never did, except to go out in the morning for the *L.A. Times* and bacon, a sweetroll for Lea, contraceptive cream. When exams came he made love right through them, and that was nearly one month later during which time he had

learned that Lea had the strongest fingers of any woman he
had ever known and that they could do anything, make anything, touch any nerve in his body. Sometimes from the bed
he'd watch her coax long-necked decanters from amorphous
damp mounds of porcelain. Sometimes he'd let her knead at
him, tug at him, explore every hump and ridge of his own
body he'd never been aware of as separate from the rest. Lea's
unelegant fingers taught him things about his separate parts
he couldn't have imagined on his own, and then when they
were done gathered him together again so that, wordless as
always with desire, he'd do for her the only thing he could for
her, which she would take as if it were enough, though of
course for her it never would be.

III.

THE LORENZ Hotel Saloon had been declining for years from
its original red finery and gilt to its current seedy decadence,
until now only longtime patrons continued to go there, fond
and stubborn and proud as hell to drink with others like
themselves; and so it was with some surprise that Norm,
complete with his purpose, found himself sitting next to a girl
he'd never seen before, what he might have called, if he called
people that, a punk, with strawlike hair, dyed white, and
dressed in a short black skirt. She giggled. In spite of himself
Norm responded with lust, but he tried to look annoyed because in that bad light and from the bright-lit lobby where he'd
entered he had for an instant mistaken her for Lea. They were
the same size, and Lea often dressed in black. By the time
Norm sat beside her, he knew she was just another stray but
he'd set his path already and couldn't circumvent it. The bartender brought him whiskey and draft. Again, the girl giggled.
Norm nodded to have her served too, and it doubly annoyed
him that she was drinking daiquiris.

Half pleased, it seemed, half despondent, the girl watched the blender blend. Only her eyes were bright. When the drink came, she sipped at it eagerly and then, as if obliged to show her gratitude with conversation, turned to Norm for the first time and asked him where he was from.

"Me?" Norm said. "Right here."

"Fuck that," the girl said. "Nobody's from here. Look around you."

Norm, who felt like spanking her, instead told the bartender, "Shorty, tell her where I'm from."

"That man?" Shorty said. "That man is a local man. Hang around, you'll see. That man farts like a true Montana man."

Shorty chuckled. The girl grinned suddenly, first to him and then even more broadly to Norm, who in spite of his heightened sensibilities just then and deeply suspicious nature, found the darkened undercast of her uneven teeth, obviously weakened, more touching than not. Norm has such healthy teeth. And when he looked again he saw she was not more than twenty, with a scar at the corner of one eye that could only have been the result of some calculated act of violence. Under her black sweater she was wearing something with a metallic thread running through it and some sequins in a pattern. On her feet she wore dirty white sneakers and one orange and one electric blue crew sock. Because everything else seemed clear and inevitable, so did the unexpected rush of tenderness Norm felt for the girl.

"So how," he said, to show her he forgave her, "did you end up here? Missoula's not exactly on the throughway."

"Bus broke down," she said. "I'm on my way from Minneapolis to Portland and the goddamn bus breaks down." This time when she smiled it was shyly. "I have a sister there. She's married, but it's cool. She works in a bank and doesn't have kids."

The girl touched her lip. Norm glanced from her to the mural

behind the bar in which a miner on his knees was holding up
a gold pan to a woman. The miner's arms reached just below
the woman's breasts. There was a pleading look on his face.
Norm, familiar with the same look on his own face, felt about
those breasts, so round and white and massive, like moons,
and those bloodred nipples just beyond the miner's reach, the
way he'd always felt about a certain hound he'd had that was
run over while chasing a bitch in heat. What he'd felt was
admiration and absolute, unending devotion. He'd loved them
more than any real woman's. Now he couldn't keep from
staring at the pattern of sequins on the girl's chest.

"I'd have done anything to get out of Minneapolis," she
said. "You know Minneapolis. It's cold."

IV.

LEA IS the kind of woman women love. What I mean is how
she is soft, and elusive, and aggressively affectionate, not so
much verbal as visual, and pretty in a way she herself would
disparage, with a long thin mouth and pale skin. She would
have been a preschool teacher, but somewhere in college discovered ceramics, the intricate mysteries of color. From muddy
earth tones she moved on to greens and blues, then to purple,
the odd yellow, and finally to reds so exotic and expensive she
never could sell what she made for as much as it cost. Red
glazes burn hot and may crack. Lea, who loved the thrill of it,
worked for years with such zealous concentration that by the
time she met Norm she could throw vases so thin they seemed
translucent and so perfectly red they seemed on fire. The
shelves of her garage, behind where she slept and ate, were
cluttered with her work – squat bowls, long-necked urns, delicate geometric-shaped boxes in which she kept ginseng,
crushed rose petals, eucalyptus seeds, cloves. When Norm
removed the lids, she sighed with pleasure, for Lea, who had

spent her life moving back and forth across the country, had never had a lover from Montana.

Ask Lea about her family. "What family?" she'll say. "I'm an orphan. I am my own woman." Maybe it's not easy for her but it's perfectly straightforward. Norm hasn't been that fortunate. On a wood box in Norm's bedroom for thirteen years he's kept an almost luminescent creamy bird's egg he thinks may have come from an eagle.

There are things in the life of almost every person, and what couldn't I tell you about Norm – his troubles, his raptures; the time his mother left, saying they could take their farts and live like pigs for all she cared, and then came back; or the time his father caught him with that migrant field worker two times as old as he was when he was still in grade school; or the time he and his girl tried to cross the swollen Clark Fork higher than they'd ever seen to where, for once, they might have been alone, but instead the girl slipped and nearly drowned. It's all, as much as daily life permits, accurate and moving. But what would you do with information like that? You'd look for significance in drowning. And the true thing is Norm felt about the girl about what he'd be expected to feel: he liked her and was sorry but what the hell, nature was nature and he'd try it all again. Wheareas with his grandfather things were a little bit different.

And this is history: how toward the end of the previous century a young man cut his ties in Baltimore and headed west. Lean and still a little pale, what did he want, in boots that didn't quite fit, without a hat brimmed broad enough? "An acre of land," he told Norm a hundred times when Norm was still a boy, "a good fifth of whiskey, two or three shots a year at a grizzly." The young man darkened, toughened, wore his boots in. Not right off but over time he had his drunks, he shot his bears, and then he married wisely. The acre and his woman multiplied. The land became a passion. Still, there never was enough to make him or his family rich even three-quarters of a century later when suddenly land values sky-rocketed, but enough, he always said, to raise his family on, to work with his son, enough to come to love it in a certain way, the way it always was, and to pass that feeling down to his late passion, Norm. I say *love* because that's how they felt. Gray, rough, and taciturn, even so he was tender with the boy. But men are less constant than land and eventually, without warning, Norm's grandfather died of a stroke while the white cow calved and Norm attended. It was a breech birth and Norm had to reach his hands in and pull the sticky creature out and steady it and find the mother's teat for it, and all the time inside the house his grandfather lay dying. Afterwards the family tried to look on the bright side, glad that both cow and calf lived, but still they were forced to sell off almost half the land to pay for the inheritance. First they auctioned what they could, and then they sold the land. At eighteen, the same age his grandfather was when he left the East forever, Norm went down to the river and cried.

Years later to Lea he says, "I should have stopped it."

"How could you?" she says.

"I should have chained myself to every tree there was and isn't anymore."

As for the girl in the bar, she calls herself Deirdre. Not on schedule but several days later she made it to Portland where she doesn't get a job in any bank.

v.

NORM had no clear idea what law school would do for him but for twenty-three years he watched the land that meant more to him than any human being or feeling bought, sold, and ravaged until just to get to the river from his father's house he had to drive five miles, circling back, or trespass through people's landscaped yards, the world as he had known it utterly transformed. Whole stands of cottonwoods were cut away. Ancient elk herds disappeared. Wild raspberries died back. From pain Norm passed to anger and finally to resolution, which because he blamed it all on California he had to go there somehow, like a test. Lea just wasn't something he planned.

"What did you plan?" she asked him once.

Norm shrugged. "They were all from California, it seemed, the investors, the developers, even the shrinks. I hated them and I hated their children. They weren't like me when I was young. They squabbled over Frisbee games and littered fast food wrappers."

"But if you hated them," Lea said.

"You hate, and you hate. I wanted to make them pay, and the only way I knew how was to find out who they were."

What Norm really wanted was to legislate cleanliness and a changeless world with strict boundaries that could never be undone, so of course he recognized the futility of his desire almost as soon as he began. Lea eased him out of law school without his hardly noticing. And as long as he didn't, everything was fine.

Norm had some money, Lea had her work, and they were careful with each other as only those who do not understand what they are risking can be. Each time they touched it was as if they never had before, with a kind of amazement and grace, like a benediction or admission of inevitable loss. Not her sex but her strange and overwhelming lightness delighted Norm who felt so heavy with his male body and his anger and his past. Lea dismissed her past, dismissed everything, in fact, but nuclear holocaust, her ceramics, and Norm. About the first she felt, like all of us, quite powerless. To the second she devoted all her time. And to the third, to Norm himself, she gave her body and her spirit absolutely, making herself be ready for him just as he wanted whenever he wanted, and she made him want her. Sometimes as she worked she'd make a half-animal sound in her throat that echoed every longing Norm had ever had. Sometimes she'd come to him leaving a half-finished urn on the wheel. But what Norm found so sweet and inexplicable he almost couldn't bear it was the way she had of fashioning small animals from clay as they talked. Her fingers hardly moved. One barely conscious pinch here, another there. Norm watched the antelope or hummingbird take shape, and always he wanted to stop it for he knew when she was done she would crush it in her fist.

VI.

THE NATURE of stories is that you can make them however you like, adding this, amending that, changing the order, whatever, and yet in the end they will seem long determined without you. Norm believes this, just as he believes the same is true of life, and so when after still another daiquiri the girl, Deirdre, turned to him and said, "Do you know anywhere to go? You know, just to talk, or like that," he gave himself up to her as if she'd been part of his plan all along. And in some sense she had been. He would need a witness after all, someone to prove for him what he had to prove to Lea. He tipped Shorty and they left together, Deirdre and Norm. She was giggling. He moved with a stern direction of body only a man of his size can affect.

When they got to Norm's camper Deirdre started to remove her sweater, and though it was May, just a year after Norm had met Lea, it was cold yet and Deirdre shivered.

"Not here," Norm said.

Deirdre put her sweater back on. They started driving south down the freeway. Out of town, the moon, just past its halfway mark, provided enough light to expose them both had they looked at each other, but they didn't. To the west black humps of hills, close enough to touch, were silhouetted against still blacker mountain peaks; to the east a black expanse of valley slid out to the river, one startling silver shaft that appeared and disappeared between clumps of cottonwoods, and then more black mountains, odd unsubstantial shapes as solemn and inevitable as if they were bound to the night that way forever. There were clouds too, the farthest edge of a storm, which blew across the sky, sporadically obscuring the moon, light. After seven miles Norm turned east down a dirt road. Almost at once they entered trees, whose branches inscribed broad arches above them in the darkness.

Deirdre hugged herself. "Back roads at night always give me the willies."

"You don't know the half of it," Norm said.

They came to a one-lane wood bridge and crossed it. The road on the other side of the river curved out through a field, then back to follow the bank. Everything smelled damp and rich.

"You know," Deirdre said, "anywhere is fine."

Norm switched to four-wheel drive to negotiate mud. "My grandfather..." he said.

"Do you have to?" Deirdre said. "I mean I just thought we'd make love."

They rounded a bend in the river and just on the other side a rural subdivision sprawled, punctuating the wilderness with lights and the uneven shapes of houses, cars.

"God," Deirdre said, "people actually live out here?"

And for the first time Norm touched her, just above the elbow, his fingers circling her thin arm a little too hard. She caught her breath. He eased the truck farther down the road until once again both sides of the river were clear and uninhabited, restored to their natural grace. There was such a look of concentration about him Deirdre stared with something like fear, something like lust. The river narrowed, turning white and frothy. Then Norm stopped. In a clearing to the left the new bare scaffolding of a house stood, floor without ceiling, roof without walls, huge. The pale lumber seemed almost white, almost to glimmer. Just begun, it was as if complete: where there would be windows there were frames, where rooms divided posts marked the places. Around them the night was perfectly still.

"Weird," Deirdre said when Norm said nothing.

"No," Norm said, "here. Right here."

VII.

WHEN Norm was eleven years old he had curly carrot-red hair and freckles so thick they depressed him. Other children made fun of him. He had grown up too fast and in all the wrong places and was, as a result, odd looking and clumsy. It was not a good year. Later, of course, he will make up a story to tell Lea. In it there will be a yellow table washed with sunlight, and him, freshly scrubbed, sitting there eating jam and bread.

"Sunny Boy jam," he will say to Lea. "You know the brand?"

Lea will shake her head no.

"Sunny Boy strawberry jam," Norm will say, "has a little redheaded boy with freckles on its label, grinning from ear to ear. I just sat there with my jam and bread staring at that little boy until it dawned on me that if he could be happy so could I."

Well maybe that happened. Maybe Norm sat at a yellow table in the sun one summer morning. And maybe that's how he felt. Lea believed him anyway, so what the hell. Naturally, though, his family was concerned. Norm cried himself to sleep at night. He didn't bring home friends after school.

That autumn snow came early, thick and destructive to fences made brittle by the season before. Almost every night Norm's grandfather drove out to check them, and often Norm rode with him. One night they drove out just at dusk, down along the bottom road, out along the west fence toward the river. Norm was pretending to watch for breaks, but the world was so white and so gray he couldn't concentrate on anything but his own unhappiness: he would never grow up, he would never fall in love. When his grandfather stopped, startled, Norm turned. His grandfather was staring out over the water toward the eastern mountains.

"There," he said in a low voice. "Over there, Norm. There."

Norm looked but saw nothing. His grandfather took his hand and pointed with it so that Norm could sight down his finger. Even so Norm looked for a long time without seeing the buck outlined against the row of trees, blackened prematurely by the passing off of light, across the river. In the silence between the man and the boy they could hear the rush of the river, only partially frozen.

At eleven Norm was not yet large enough to handle any gun with ease, so his grandfather stood beside him, steadying the barrel. Neither said anything, but when Norm was ready his grandfather pressed his shoulder and Norm pulled the trigger. Half a second later, in the distance, the buck fell.

Norm skinned that buck the way he skinned so many that came after, full of love and awe for the animal but also with a sense of his own enormous power. The thing that had been living, more beautiful almost than the mountains of Montana, was made dead by his own hand, which even as it cut and tore caressed. There were moments when he and the carcass seemed one. In later years, as if to consecrate the union, he gnawed on fresh meat while he worked. The taste of the blood ran deep in his throat and he wanted nothing more than to have it in him always.

VIII.

NORM thought he would try writing articles about how the West was lost.

"Write about the demonstration," Lea said. "Make us famous."

Norm went to the library and researched land distribution and mineral rights. Lea stumbled on his books. They argued.

"Do you know why the elk disappear?" Norm said.

"So what, am I to blame?" Lea said.

"People build houses where they used to graze, and the elk are so timid they starve in the hills."

Lea laid her head in his lap. "Norm, please."

It went on like that. Lea couldn't stand to listen to him because no matter what he said it was so imbued with pain she couldn't navigate the distance it put between them. She heard of a job for a park gardener.

"You'd like it," she said. "They have ducks and growing things there, Norm – flowers, trees. Listen to me, Norm."

"There's this man," Norm said, "who's bought the land across the river from my father's place. He's building a house, a big house. Ten thousand square feet, people say. Ten thousand square feet of Renaissance Tudor in front of the Bitterroots, imagine that."

Lea couldn't. It was too foreign to her, not just the Tudor but the mountains themselves. She reached for a piece of clay and started pinching at it.

"Don't," Norm said.

"Oh hell," she said.

She made a fish, she made a swan, she made an elk and lined them up along the bed. She made a hawk, she made a goat, she made a marmot.

"The whole state of Montana is being ruined," Norm said.

"Yeah, well California's finished."

"That's no answer."

"That's progress. I'm sorry."

She made a horse, she made a squirrel, she made a goose.

Norm said, "There used to be buffalo out where we lived."

Lea made a buffalo. "Five or six domestic head that had more or less gone wild. And we had black bears, each spring with cubs." Lea made a black bear with two cubs. "Antelope played on our range."

Lea sighed. "They just let them run around wild like that?"

Norm moved to put aside the animals and take her to him.

"Don't," she said, reaching for the goat.

"No, you don't," Norm said. "You know how that infuriates me."

But Lea took the goat and crushed it, and then the fish, and then the hawk. "They're mine. I make them. I do what I want."

Norm didn't understand. They were so beautiful to him, and it was such a waste. For Norm saw nothing in the clay itself, damp pale mounds where she worked. He grabbed Lea's wrist to stop her.

"If that's how you feel, prove it," she said. "Do something," she said. And then she took the bear and cubs and placed them in Norm's hand and forced his fingers closed around them and squeezed until they both wept.

IX.

"WE HAVE to find a bedroom," Norm said. "I'm not going to do it except in a bedroom."

"But how can you tell which is a bedroom?"

Deirdre stood outside the huge unfinished structure, staring up at it as though it were evil, and for an instant refused to go in. But Norm took the ramp in two steps and then turned back to her, who let him take her hand and pull her up beside him. Inside their steps echoed as they passed from room to room. There were so many of them, rudely marked out, connected in places by rough scaffolding. Norm led Deirdre through what might have been a hall up a slatted ramp through what might have been a bathroom or a closet to a largish room which must

have been a bedroom that led onto a balcony, just the flooring
down. From the moon light spilled in, making the darkness of
shadows darker. Deirdre moved to blend back into them.
Norm walked out onto the balcony where, without the rails
built, he felt both exposed and omnipotent, as if, as long as he
stayed there, up above the world staring out across the river,
nothing could ever cross him, and he didn't yet think about
coming down.

"Be careful," Deirdre said, softly, behind him.

"Shh," Norm said. "See that solitary light off there by itself?
That's where my father lives." He paused. "And here I killed
my first deer, where we are."

Deirdre moved back toward the darkest corner of the bedroom and letting her back slide down the smooth side of a
two-by-four, sat and drew her knees up, hugging them close
to her chest. Where Norm stood he looked bigger than he was,
and sturdier, his hands turned out from his thighs, his oddly
rectangular head at a level with the moon. A sound came from
Deirdre, almost a whimper. Norm turned.

"Look," she said. "I meant what I said. All this family stuff
gives me the creeps. You know, I just thought maybe we could
screw or something."

"That's what we did too, at the end."

"What?" Deirdre said.

"Fucked," Norm said. "Over and over, as if that was all that
was left or the only way we had. And we had to do it. We
couldn't stop ourselves."

Deirdre hugged herself tighter, her hands, where they grip-
ped her upper arms, turning white at the knuckles and the
veins showing through. Norm wished he had the bear and her
two cubs now, the way he held them all through their lovemaking that night, because though Lea's fingers were strong his
were stronger. In the morning, in bright light, she found them

in the bed and laughed. "Couldn't do it, could you Norm," she said. And then she ground them down to dust, grating one against the other as he watched.

But Deirdre wasn't Lea and when Norm took her finally, there, high and deep inside the skeleton of the house he despised, it was without passion or grace. Nothing she could have said or done could have alleviated the loss he felt, the emptiness and yet unconsummated righteousness. She drew away from him almost as soon as he was done, and he went down to the camper, saying nothing but moving as if having rid himself of that, he could rid himself at last of the other.

When he came back Deirdre was dressed and ready to go, and I suppose that given who she was she could have had no way of knowing what he meant with the gasoline and torch he brought back with him.

Norm said, "I want you to watch."

"No," Deirdre said.

Norm started spreading gasoline.

"My mother is crazy. My father is dead."

"Shut up," Norm said, and led her downstairs. "I just said to watch, that's all."

"No," Deirdre said, but without conviction or hope of persuasion. Then for a long time she said nothing. And when Norm lit and raised the torch and the fire started she didn't try to fight it either. She turned and ran.

Norm stayed in the house for awhile, feeling the heat grow at his back and watching her, framed by the lumber, run down the road, the both of them as if surprised — she by terror, he by himself. Who was she, he wondered, and why had he brought her here with him? But as the flames took hold he lost interest, and besides she disappeared anyway. Soon he was forced outside, first to the near ground, then little by little back toward his truck. Each of the supports was licked now by flames, their tongues flicking up at the night filled with hunger and what seemed like love. Norm, who felt himself to be in a subtle state of mind, felt also very much like them, never so beautiful, never so full of absolute power. In the end he went down on his knees, not to pray but to feel the earth at his center, firm and, as he returned it to itself, once again not transgressed against, and thus made holy.

x.

LEA, I should say, has another life now and though when Norm wrote and sent clippings and news photographs she wanted more than anything to come to him, she knew this other life lay before her even then and so just never answered, sent not one mortal word. Well, two people like that should never have met. I mean that. There are people who, no matter how deeply they may come to love each other, can only over time cause great harm. And it's so arbitrary anyway. A bus stops and there's no other place to sit; a nuclear power plant goes up and a random crowd gathers to protest. Still, I wouldn't have you think this is a case of opposites. It's a case of curiosity and longing combined with a mutual stubbornness so entrenched they found, Norm and Lea, that only in their lovemaking could they circumvent it. And certainly they might have kept themselves to that, but love is like fire: it follows its own path outward till it dies. Or like fish, which also grow and grow until they also die, too large to be supported by the simple workings of their own bodies.

In the beginning Lea used to ask Norm what color Montana was. Norm never understood. "You know," she said, "the trees, you have trees there, and mountains. Lakes, rivers, valleys, that sort of thing." Norm, at a loss, could only answer, "Gray." For to him, who despite his eventual union with God has no decent sense of color, that's what the mountains were, granite, and the sky that hung low over them nine months of the year. It took Norm too long to think *red*, and by the time he did it was over.

Now, of course, none of that matters, for a man who finds God at twenty-nine passes directly from post-adolescence to acceptance, absolved in one stroke of all the usual doubt, guilt, and anger. I'm not trying to justify anything. God is ephemeral and enigmatic and comes to each of us in such different ways, as often as not in disguise. It's like Lea fashioning one of her animals, a reflex she performs because she can't not. But again, there is something so outrageously autonomous and other about what she has made when she's done she also can't not destroy it. I think Norm would agree, though since that other March day on the riverbank he's also passed beyond the need for self-reflection.

Here is what happened. For three inconsolable years Norm sought after Lea. He wrote, but she never answered. He went back to California to try and track her down, but she had moved. And she didn't have parents that he knew of so there was no help there. What he didn't know, and never will I guess, was that Lea started making things she didn't imagine, she just, like her animals, made. Eventually, she had to move to have space for her ceramics – huge three-foot urns, serenely curved and infinitely white except where forked coiling tendrils of red started thin at the bottoms, engulfing their necks. You could probably construct some meaning from that, but then maybe you couldn't. Lea still finds herself wordless before what she's done, and Norm would find it in himself now to smash them all without hesitation or remorse. Because though it took three years, that second time he walked five miles up the river the wind and the water converged in such a way he'd never heard it like that before. *Confess*, they seemed to say to him, and so for the second time in his life Norm went down on his knees and confessed. That night in the fire he'd thought he had seen Lea; now he knew that what he'd seen was God. And now he saw God everywhere, still does in fact. Like Lea, he can't not.

Like Lea too, Norm can't forget. The knowledge is always in him these days, not so much a promise as a conviction, only sometimes it troubles him. Sometimes he walks up the river again and no matter what the season is, the land there seems invulnerable and sacrosanct. What troubles him is not that, it's that perhaps it's not enough to embrace God on the stones of a river. If you listen you can almost hear the water, feel the cool earth beneath your own knees, see the Indian paintbrush poking out from under brush, for it's late summer now and there are wildflowers. The tenderness of the flowers is almost more than Norm can bear. This is not a thought, it's a feeling: Norm has come to conceive of himself as having sinned and he would be like them, untainted. In his heart he plays with ideas of atonement: he will not think of Lea, he will forbear. And he wonders. Lately more than anything he wonders what the man in the rebuilt Tudor mansion, completed two years now and every bit as garish as Norm had been afraid, would say to him if Norm would bring himself and his God to him, as I think perhaps he will, not today and not tomorrow but soon.

A Scrap of Green Silk

I.

Wнат I have to say about that is this: Eva knew what she was doing, right from the very start, but she couldn't help herself. Such a roundness of body she had, not at all like other women, firm and with something inevitable, like sculpture, about it, but at the same time plastic, unpredictable.

Eva moved onto our block when the Johnsons moved out.

"Twenty-five years we've lived here," Mr. Johnson said when he said I could have the early scallions. "We raised our children here."

Our block was all little houses so it's not, as you may think, that they felt the old place was too big for them, that they were just rattling around. No, the Johnsons were old and they had their ways, and Eva, like the rest of us, was young. Young is relative. We were all old enough to have a little money; and we were still so young that our interests, even then, centered more on music than on anything so grown-up as, say, children, procreation.

"Kids," Dan said. "What did I ever give my parents but grief?"

"They can blow me up in the nuclear holocaust," Lucy said. "But they won't get any child of mine."

Charlene put another record on and wondered, out loud, why we talked about such things. As far as she was concerned adults were adults and children were children and she was grateful enough, finally, to be among the former.

So there were high-tech stereos on our block, and when it was cold you could hear them through closed doors and windows, and when it was warm we cranked them up and sat half-clothed on our little lawns where in rare quiet moments we also read not the Bible but books about women and poetry from Nicaragua. We were a mixed and difficult generation and I, for one, was glad when the Johnsons left, though of course I felt guilty. But I felt less guilty then than when they carried their groceries in, him with the bags, her with her cane, small people hunched over daily life and the arbitrary props and barriers it gave them. It was like that for all the two years I had lived there. They drove up in their long, noisy, light gray car and shuffled from their driveway to their front door without ever looking over at, for instance, Lucy and me drinking beer on her front porch and listening, half awake, to Peruvian flutes she'd taped in the Andes, eerie and sweet. On Sundays, while we lay in bed, heavy with the aftermath of alcohol and sex, the Johnsons went to church. They shopped on Tuesdays. Even so, Mrs. Johnson brought me cherries from their tree in the summer and offered I should help myself to roses from her bushes.

"You have so few," she said, a little shyly. "Do you want to see my iris? More like an orchid, my prize iris."

I went to see her iris and duly admired it, but never helped myself to her roses. That would have been too much like admitting my mother was right: I should have married when the other girls in my hometown did, I should have had children of my own. Eva was such a relief. She was a painter and, as I say, round, in her pink and yellow skirts and green go-aheads. The roses were blooming when she moved in. Lucy and I picked a huge bouquet from Eva's own new yard and hung it from Eva's new eaves.

LUCY lived with Charlene but they weren't lovers. This was difficult for Lucy, but Charlene said, "Whoever I live with, I make sure it's platonic."

Dan said, "She's lying. She just won't hurt Lucy's feelings. But Charlene's no dyke, and you and I both know it."

"Don't be rude," I said, and fetched another beer for him, another glass of wine for me. We weren't counting. Dan was moody. He would drink, and did, until I kicked him out, back to his side of our duplex.

That was the spring just before Eva came and just after the winter Dan took up with Charlene. All winter I kept my front thermal drapes wide open and stood there, watching for him, watching for her, crossing up the street, crossing down the street, plowing through knee-deep snow toward the other's untidy bedroom. As the weeks passed and the snowpack receded, drawing back from around the first stalks of grass and tiny, low, pale flowers, they shed, Charlene and Dan, one by one their outer garments until even I was forced to admire the infinitely touching thrust of her small breasts, bare beneath her cotton T-shirts. I'd never say Charlene wasn't beautiful. She was beautiful – not quite full-sized and precociously seductive, fey, dark, with the kind of exaggerated face that in the wrong light or angle would seem just this side of distorted. But the light was never wrong, nor the angle, for the high, clean arch of Charlene's cheekbones and brows, the queer inverted sweep of her nose. And the color of her eyes was something in between jade green and a yellower moss. It wasn't contacts, though I thought that for awhile. Everybody did. Dan was the last to admit her beauty, uncanny though it was, was all Charlene's natural own. When he did, he still insisted such beauty held no interest for, nor power over him.

A man who claims not to want beautiful women may convince you for awhile if you're not beautiful; he may even be telling the truth. But no matter how much you may care for that man, you test him in the end. You're that way.

"Listen," I told Dan when the time came, "let's just be friends now. Let's see how that goes."

He cupped my chin the way I used to love it and nodded once and then went home next door where I heard him put some water on to boil, kick his boots off, turn the stereo on low.

I'M NOT telling things this way to confuse you about time. We're talking almost three years here, during which time our configurations shifted with a curious fluidity that in any other circumstances would have been alarming. As it was, we prided ourselves on our circumstance. If I got it on with Dan for a year, you should have heard my explanation: not fate, not chemistry, but the random accident by which, on the day I moved in, my grandmother's trunk jammed shut and locked, and there hasn't been a key since long before she died. Dan worked at it with a nail. By the time he got it open we were drinking.

"It's good he lives next door," I told Lucy three months later. "I could never live with him. He's insatiable."

"Charlene's a good roommate," Lucy said. "She's almost never home."

I knew that, of course. Even then I watched the block. But I wondered. Lucy had her fingers at her hairline.

"Still," I tried again, "it's nice he's so close. I've got my freedom without having to get lonely."

"Do you get lonely?" Lucy said. She sounded eager. That wasn't what I meant. I mumbled something noncommittal. Embarrassed, she offered me something to eat.

"Lucy?" I said.

"What the hell," she said. "Loneliness is just an attitude, don't you think?"

I didn't, I still don't, I never have: only did I say as much to Lucy then? Whatever I might have said, she circumvented it, putting on music, slicing cheese on a round blond board, saying something about a tapestry she planned.

"I've sent for the silk," she said softly. "I've never woven with silk before."

After awhile Charlene came home. It was cold that day but the skirt she was wearing was sheer and showed her legs through, slim above her boots, and she had that energy by which we both knew she had just come from making love. Sex charged Charlene. Dan, fed up with the intimate demands of my languor, explained this to me later, but of course I knew as much beforehand. Everything about Charlene was perfectly apparent. On this particular day, when she had been with her identity professor, she went straight into the bathroom to wash her face, we heard her, and brush her "impossible" hair. Then she came back with a cup of coffee and kissed Lucy blandly on the cheek.

To me she said, "Did you know women form their identities in different ways than men. We're more fluid, did you know? We can fuse."

"INDONESIAN," Lucy, flushed, said, holding up a piece of fabric, red but with so many different colors woven through it – peacock, emerald, gold – I had to concentrate to keep them separate, not to lose them in a vertigo of dye.

"What?" Dan said, as usual not all that pleased to see her.

"It's from Indonesia," Lucy said. "But look how close it is to Guatemalan."

"I haven't the faintest idea what you're talking about," Dan said.

"Fabric," I said. "She's talking about the fabric." To Lucy I said, "Do you want to stay for dinner?"

Lucy was staring at Dan. "You came over just to show us a piece of cloth?" he said. The professor's blue car was parked down the street. "You're cooking tonight," I said, "aren't you?" to Dan.

Dan motioned to me to follow him into the kitchen. Lucy had a bright look in her eyes I didn't want to face either. Now she was staring at me.

"I don't love her, you know," she said, a little too calmly.

But when Charlene came over later, after we had eaten and were well into our drinking and the blue car down the street had been gone for half an hour, it was the way it always was, the way no matter what we said when she wasn't there Charlene would turn it into something different when she was. If we were tired and she showed up, suddenly we weren't anymore. If we didn't want to drink, she did, and could convince us easily with a giggle or half-calculated touch of her hand. There was much that was nice in those evenings we so often spent together. Charlene, small as she was, would sit in our laps—Lucy's, mine, Dan's—and pet us as a child would, and despite how we might feel at other times, our hearts would go out to her then, though Dan and I knew how little it meant. Or I did. Dan, as you know, had his fling with her later. And Lucy had her innocence, her unspeakable desire.

II.

THERE are people you fall in love with and people you don't. And it happens maybe once, maybe two or three times a year that you do and when it does sometimes you know it but more often you don't because there are rules for these things, not to mention right and wrong. Dan I argued with and slept with and had my own feelings about but finally did not love, I think, a failing that, in retrospect, I realize was as much my fault as his, and yes, I know now too I might have changed things if I hadn't felt so strongly he wanted me to be too much like him. How he put it was: "Given my preference, I'd take a relationship all on my own terms," and Dan, in addition, had no decent sense of irony. As for Charlene, she was already the recipient of far more devotion than is good for any person. This is not a confession, just something that happened, as all of this happened, one way or another. Because who I fell in love with that year was Lucy. I couldn't understand how other people didn't.

Lucy was a weaver who had an uncanny instinct for fabrics — wool, cotton, silk — though you'd never have known it from looking at her. She liked always to dress simply, in jeans and her brother's old shirts, or a pair of dark lavender sweat pants and some kind of T-shirt. The sweat pants brought out a character in Lucy people often found disturbing. In them she moved not like her sterner self, but like a happy, clownish mime, bending her body at odd, inappropriate angles, gesturing this way and that with her foot. Lucy had beautiful feet. She had double-jointed toes and arches that rose and curved like the serenest edge of an egg. So if she was extravagant in what she wore, it was in her socks.

"Socks," she told me once. "You can tell a lot about a person from a person's socks."

Hers, not always matched, were striped or hand-knit or with contrasting heels and toes, and the colors she chose were like those of the flags we tied one March day to the Japanese locust in her front yard. If I tied a green one up, she tied purple next to it; if I chose yellow, she chose red. They were remnants she'd got at a store that sold silk from all over the world — China, Italy, France. Lucy could tell just by feeling a scrap where it had been spun, where, by holding it up to the light, the cloth had actually been dyed. By midafternoon the tree was transformed, trailing its bright offerings up into that almost spring day like some kind of Oriental shrine. Afterwards, we sat under it drinking whiskey and beer and turning our faces to the incipient warmth of a sun that had for months lain dormant behind the gray sky of the season.

"You can smell it first," she said.

"What?"

"The coming on of spring."

And indeed I did smell something, though if I had been asked, I would have guessed Charlene's perfume lingering in Lucy's dark lavender pants.

How you look at a person depends, I suppose, on your predilections. Me, for instance: I'd never made love to a woman and had no inclination to. Lucy wasn't even physically my type. She was pale and stout and, except for her feet and the way she maneuvered her legs, almost entirely lacking in any normal sense of grace. Even her henna-stained hair was chopped awkwardly off, too short and always too red. Her shoulders curved over her chest, one slightly higher than the other. Her left arm, as if of its own, sought the back of any chair and clung there grimly. She couldn't keep her hands from her face. Whatever uncommon sympathy she engendered in me came from something beyond what you might normally expect — an ingenuous abruptness, a habit of looking straight at you as if to determine exactly what you felt and how. Really, that's what Dan found unnerving in her.

"I can't get any distance," he complained.

"You're one," I said, "to talk about distance."

"Let's not get into that again," he warned.

And for once he was right. We'd been through all that so many times already and come up every time against the same dead ends. Dan made love to bring me to him, not the other way around. He talked sports when I wanted to talk us. And as soon as, in spite of myself, I developed an affinity for a

particular team, he'd switch allegiances, just like that. Whereas
with Lucy, if I admired the way a certain rookie pitcher pitched,
so solemn and intent, she'd watch him too and see exactly
what I meant. Not that we either of us cared about baseball.
Just that we saw the same slice of the forearm, the identical
hook of the wrist.

EVA DROVE a Volkswagen. I drove a Volkswagen. Her car
was exactly like mine, spattered with gray primer and dented
on all the same fenders, only green. But she moved her things
in as if, if she no longer had money, she once did, with a style
calculated to let us know that were there any question of
intruding it was we, not she, who were in error. And indeed I
did watch her all afternoon. Every time she went inside she
ducked around the roses Lucy and I had hung for her arrival,
never stopping once to smell or touch them.

"That's what I like in a woman, is class," Dan said behind
me.

I wanted to tell him Mr. Johnson promised me the early
scallions. I wanted to tell him to shut up. But he was there, like
old good friends, and this was habit. Later, I sliced eggplant
for pasta, but in my distraction sautéed it on too low a flame,
not even caring that the uneven cubes turned gray and wilted
as they just soaked up oil. To compensate, I tossed in extra red
peppers. Dan swore and drank too many beers, as if it were
deliberate and I ruined everything.

"You never made it hot like this before. What are you, jeal-
ous?"

"So get Charlene to cook for you. I thought we were supposed to be friends."

"Leave Charlene out of this. She's busy. You just burned my
tongue."

"Aw Dan, cut it out," I pleaded. "You've got things your way
now. So be civil and eat. Or go home."

He helped himself to seconds and said, "If it bothers you, my being here, just say so."

That night Eva came over with a candle. "I made this," she said. "I'm Eva."

"Come in," I said.

"Light the candle," Dan said.

I did, and Eva said nothing.

Eva ate some pasta without making any fuss, and Dan finally had enough beer. We exchanged the usual pleasantries. Her cheeks were full, with a perpetual, grainy blush to them, the same color as her chest, which rose in a splendid expanse above the low scoop of her blouse. It was well into the evening before she finally told us she was from back east but came here on instinct because of the mountains.

"You know about mountains," she said.

Dan was studying the elegant line of her chin. I was studying the rings she wore on every finger and the several gold bracelets at each wrist.

At last Dan said, "Yeah, the mountains. I know."

Eva took a pouch of marijuana from her pocket and started rolling joints, thin and pretty in pink papers, then gave one each to Dan, to herself, to me. I left mine on the table.

"It's Colombian," she told me in a low voice, "the flower."

"What do you know," I asked Dan, "about mountains?"

Dan lit his joint and wouldn't look at me.

"I love them," Eva said. "They're so spiritual and wild, don't you think."

"Dan's in real estate," I said, which was only half true. Dan was still studying for his license.

"Are you?" said Eva.

"He speculates," I said. "He's got his eye on some new subdivisions. You should see them."

"I would like to," Eva said.

But I didn't think she would.

PEOPLE who want to be artists without caring about art have no real sense of destiny. They think they do, but it eludes them. They think that whatever they experience is somehow realer than whatever you or I or Lucy may experience. If I eat a cookie and drink some tea that's what I do: I eat and drink. But Proust, with exactly the same kind of cookie and tea, transforms them into something exotic, unforgettable. He can because he's Proust, but what we forget is that in the lives of so many of the rest of us it's as much the moment as who we are that counts. Some people forget that more than most. And when they do they develop an aura, often mistaken for a lack of self-consciousness but really perfect solipsism, that deludes and takes in the rest of us precisely because it denies us. I said before Eva was a relief, and she was – because she had that aura. Eva, who seemed to touch everything, never even came close.

Let me give you an example. First she painted each room of the Johnson's house a different pastel color – peach, whipped egg yolk yellow, a shade of blue not ever found in nature. Then she hung her paintings and furnished the whole place with geometric-patterned pillows, large and soft and tossed into just the right corners at the right spontaneous angles. In her creamy bedroom she had a dusky rose *shiki-buton*. Only her kitchen was white.

"Like a laboratory," she said at her first party. "For my gastronomic experiments."

And indeed she served us things to eat we'd only imagined in our previous lives – garlic-smothered escargots, oysters on the half shell, French bread so sour we had to wash it down with white wine distilled from red grapes.

"They're peeled before crushing," she told Dan in private. "So the mash doesn't stain. It's pure."

"And excellent," said Dan, who was drunk.

Lucy, on the pillow next to mine, put her hand on my knee.

We were waiting for Charlene, still out with her professor. I thought about moving my knee but couldn't think how without Lucy noticing. Eva's paintings, geometric like her pillows, were the same pale colors as her walls. She's gone to so much trouble, I thought vaguely, to erase every sign of the Johnsons. In her short-sleeved red corduroy shirt, brushed thin with age and soft as flannel, Lucy wasn't saying anything. Eva's roundness disturbed her. We could have left then and maybe we should have, but Lucy had promised Charlene she would wait. All Eva's candles were scented. Oblivious of us, she kept chatting with Dan, deliberate and sure with her instinct.

At last Lucy whispered, "She's just an anachronism, that's what she is. You and I, thank God, have at least avoided that."

When I looked at Lucy in that light, I saw as if for the first time how there was nothing elegant at all about her chin. I saw how it was ugly and was, despite my affection, strangely grateful. For what I wanted in that moment was that Lucy, lumps and odd stirrings of passion and all, should stay that way forever. I wanted her chin to remain as obstinate and homely as it had always been. Because of course I already knew that she was wrong. There wasn't anything anachronistic about Eva. Eva was too clever for that.

III.

CHARLENE broke off with her professor when I broke off with Dan. Maybe she planned it, maybe not. What she told Lucy was that he, the professor, was a long-necked bourgeois; to Dan, she complained about his sexuality. Dan, as if to vindicate his gender, was first concerned, and then involved. Who am I to feel slighted? This was months before Eva, and I've tried to explain how we made ourselves believe there wasn't any bitterness between Dan and me. It's not that it wasn't allowed, it's just that it wasn't quite reasonable somehow. The true thing is the way we lived made no allowance, then or now, for such pedestrian emotions as jealousy or heartbreak. And then there were Dan's own limitations, his sweet, innocuous self.

Dan was the type who, on any given day, might get up, bake bread, lose another part-time job, call his mother long-distance but not ask for money, jog a half dozen miles, read a book on stock investments, take me out for pizza, and get, if not thoroughly, pleasantly drunk. Dan was tall and leggy and basically good-natured. Every night between five and six when the weather was good, he'd shoot baskets at the hoop on his side of our house, while inside, one apartment over, I would listen: *thump, thump, thump.* Before Charlene, I used to calculate the time between the final thump, his shower, and the moment he appeared, wet-haired and eager, at my door. After, he seemed a little quicker taking off down the street, though from where I watched he also seemed, if anything, a little better groomed. Sometimes, for her, he'd shorten his basketball hour; sometimes, I believe, he cut it altogether. And yet I swear, though there were things my evenings seemed empty without then – the guilt-free third imported beer, the pleasant extended lovemaking – had it been anyone else but Charlene, I would have been happy for them. As it was, whenever I saw him or her pass boldly toward the other's house, I felt something unfamiliar and very close to pain. And then I'd give them maybe fifteen minutes, maybe half an hour before, on impulse, calling Lucy, as casual as I could make it.

"Lucy," I'd say, "what are you doing?"

"Weaving," she would often say, or sometimes making jam, or putting henna on her hair, or watching TV, or hand-washing socks, or sometimes, the saddest, "Nothing." If Charlene was at Dan's, I'd go visit Lucy, or if Dan was at their place, we'd try to find a movie, any movie would do, or someplace to have coffee, maybe pastries. Lucy didn't want to talk about it, ever, but then I was the one who'd been jilted. I was the one who was supposed to be hurt. And so I talked about it that way, on and on for hours, to let her know, I told myself, it was all right to care. Lucy was kind and what you might call forbearing, though God knows she didn't have that in her. God knows she knew what she could care about and what she couldn't.

One night, at my place, we drank some rum Charlene gave me for Christmas.

"Don't," she said finally. "Don't you see it doesn't matter."

"But Dan's Dan," I said. "First me, then Charlene. Next month he'll find some bimbo at his new job. When we were twenty it was one thing, but now we're thirty and I can't help but think it was all a mistake."

"Charlene has been my roommate for three years," Lucy said. "I can't count the men she's been with. You can't think I let it bother me. How could I?"

What I thought was: how could you not? I myself fell in love with a man my mother went to college with when he passed through town the summer I was sixteen. Ten years later I passed through his city and fell in love all over again. If a person cares, she cares, and no matter of time or neglect will change that. Which is what I might have said, but the rum was so thick and unpredictable in my head, and Lucy held more things in reserve than I ever did with Dan. Even so I can't say what stopped me from putting my arms around her and telling her *Change your life now before it's too late,* though I can make guesses. My guess is that though I wanted to lay my head on her breasts and receive all the comfort I sensed there, I wanted to keep her off mine. This is honest. I have little, hard, sensitive breasts and probably I was afraid that one flick of Lucy's tongue would completely undo everything about my life I was trying so hard to keep then from falling apart. We drank some more and then Dan stopped by.

"Where's Charlene?" I said.

"She's at home," he said. "What are you doing here, Lucy? We thought you were at home."

"I'm drinking rum," Lucy said. "I'll call Charlene."

And so Charlene came over too, though it was almost midnight and Dan really had to keep his new job this once. "Fuck sleep," he said, as Charlene headed straight for Lucy's lap and put her arms around her where half an hour before I had wanted to put mine. "We saw such a funny movie," she said, nuzzling Lucy's neck. "It would have made you laugh."

Lucy laughed, but her hand on Charlene's thigh lay still, as if without life or desire. Dan went next door for his basketball and returned with it spinning on his finger. My own hands, with nothing to do, poured rum for everyone. It occurred to me, if we were rich, Charlene would be passing out cocaine. That was one thing she had gotten from her professor. One morning, Lucy told me, her nose had bled and bled. I tried to imagine Charlene's dainty nose bleeding. At last she got off Lucy's lap and moved over onto Dan's. And so we passed the night almost until dawn, and when I woke late in the morning Lucy and Charlene were still curled up on my floor – Charlene's head at rest on Lucy's soft belly; Lucy, wide awake, staring at the ceiling.

"She doesn't mean anything," Lucy said. "She just doesn't like sleeping alone."

"Charlene," I said, "wake up. Do you want coffee? You're late for class."

"OH SURE, they sleep together," Dan told me later, "when I'm not there. But it's nothing. Charlene likes her comforts. You can't hold that against her."

"You mean without sex?" I had to know.

"Listen, I told you, Charlene's no dyke. She gets lonely, just like you do. But she's straight."

Dan took an apple off the top of my refrigerator and bit

loudly into it, grinning. I left him in the kitchen, not knowing
what to say. He followed me out to the big front picture window where we stood for awhile, him munching, me, for some
reason I'll never understand, wanting to make love to him
more then than ever before. Instead, I imagined them together.
I imagined Charlene, who lacked defenses anyway, letting
down her hair and giving him exactly what he wanted, surren-
dering absolutely, abandoning her ego for his. Would it, I
wondered, have been that difficult? If I hadn't been so stubborn, who might we have spared? And yes, I was on the verge
of saying something when Eva, new that week, drove up and
waved at us gaily.

Dan waved back. "Now that's what I call neighborhood
improvement."

"Get out," I told him, and suddenly meant it. "Please, Dan,
tonight just leave me alone."

IV.

EVA, NOT complex or even deep, failed to make much distinction between men and women, embracing them both the
same and both with such vitality and warmth you found yourself equally, if uncharacteristically, forthcoming. I know because that's how she hugged me, from the first time to the last
time, no change. In between she came over often enough and
we listened to music and hugged. It was nice. And if I asked
her what she thought of children or nuclear holocaust or faith,
she'd look at me as if she didn't know, she'd never thought
about it. And if at night I stopped myself from calling Lucy so
much anymore, I never felt the same reserve with Eva. That
makes sense to me now. After all, I didn't love her. She smelled
of a different incense all the time. Later, I would sit by my
telephone and wait for Lucy to call me. But that was later.

The night of Eva's first party, before any of it was habit, she hugged all of us that way as we arrived. Lucy alone resisted, not so apparently that she was rude, but with a coolness I'd never have expected of her, keeping herself erect and turning one pale cheek to Eva's cordial kiss without returning one of her own. They stood apart for awhile, face to face, chatting the way my mother used to over bridge or with some date of mine while, upstairs, I tried to hide pimples, flatten my hair. Every once in awhile Lucy would turn to look at one or another of Eva's paintings, nodding as if she both understood and was in perfect agreement. But in private to me later she shrugged and said, "They look like squares and circles as far as I'm concerned."

Charlene arrived, already drunk.

"She's drunk," Dan said. "Goddammit. What the hell does she have to be drunk for."

Eva was hugging Charlene. "You're a painter," we all heard her say.

Dan, still disgruntled, said, "My ass. Ten to one she's got a trust fund. Ten to one she turns out to be a trust fund Marxist, wait and see."

"That's what you call neighborhood improvement?" I said.

But I won't say it wasn't pretty, Eva and Charlene standing in the kitchen, so white behind their ethnic tunics – Eva's in lavenders and greens, Charlene's of that Indonesian cloth Lucy showed us. Eva was large and round and her loose garment billowed with the breeze; Charlene, as always, seemed childlike in her smallness. I moved to say something to Lucy and upset her wineglass, which shattered, its long black stem an obsidian scar on the polished hardwood floor. Eva was all over with a dark towel.

"Don't worry," she kept saying. "I'll just make another."

Lucy told me later that she had. Charlene, who was there, told how Eva sat in the middle of a studio she rented and blew molten black glass from a long lead pipe. Charlene in all her life had never seen anything more beautiful or moving. I myself observed a similar performance and must confess it's true: the fluid glass, just a bubble at first, like a live thing swelled, sinuous and stretching, thinner and thinner and fading all the time from blood red to glorious pink, until, at exactly the right moment, Eva sighed and let it freeze into a solid shape, delicate and perfectly curved. And then she let it cool on a stone slab.

v.

IT WASN'T as if Dan had anything against trust fund Marxists. You know how people are. They say one thing, desire another, and eventually get either or both. Summer came, and when Charlene returned Dan to me, no worse in some respects for wear but in others a little more worn, I took him, as I always knew I would. Unlike Lucy, I need it, and I'm normal.

There are things about people you love that no matter what you would do for them if you could you just can't, not even for them. And there are people you want only the best for who, no matter what, just mess things up. Lucy got the silk and started weaving at her tapestry, but I didn't go to see it. Instead, I stood at my window and watched Charlene go back and forth from the Johnson's house, now Eva's, which was where I went too when I made myself go out, which was where I admired Eva's paintings as if in her circles and squares I saw something that of course I never did, which was where I came to contemplate her roundness, which I found, in spite of everything, unutterably seductive. As for the paintings, the same colors as her walls, in fact they made no sense to me, though Charlene explained over and over how voluptuous they were, and sensual, and close to the absolute center of things. When she was drunk, she liked to trace her finger to certain intersections in them and say, "There." Eva always served a soft white cheese with, if we wanted, champagne.

Lucy continued to weave her tapestry all through July and August, working with thousands of thin colored threads that must have made her fingers sweat, sorting them, twisting them, shuttling them, tying them. Charlene said she was weaving a tall, spreading tree, lush, with animals coupling at its base. *In the top of the tree,* she said, *there will be birds; there will be a bright yellow sun.* Charlene said it was too symbolic for her. Dan said Charlene was lying. *In it, it is night,* he said. *Lucy plans a moon, not a sun. Animals sleep at the base of the tree, and the branches above, as in winter, are barren.* Dan, a new convert to abstract art, objected to its representationalism. He preferred the old whimsical Lucy, he said, tying scraps of material up in trees. As for me, sometimes I could see her at her window, weaving. Was I curious? I'm not sure I was even curious. But of course I did not know then what I know now: that both Charlene and Dan were right, that Lucy's tapestry had two sides and each of them was different.

What the hell. This wasn't fate, this was random. So Lucy never came to Eva's, so we never went there anymore. Were we to blame? We were four hapless people, and then five, and if what we did was wrong we did it because when you're careless, as we were, each day becomes too much like any other: you wake, you go to work or not depending if you have a job, you get drunk, you go to sleep. For the whole time I lived on that block I thought it didn't matter where you slept or how. Even those nights I lay awake listening to Dan and Charlene I felt a tenderness for them and their pleasure I thought was both natural and good. And we so loved Eva's soft white cheese, her endless supply of champagne. If we missed Lucy's Peruvian flutes or her stern and critical eye, Charlene was still sweet to hold on our laps and, in Eva's presence, we found it impossible to acknowledge what we'd lost. Raspberries came into season and we ate them with cream. Eva never made it to the mountains.

DAN WAS sitting on the *shiki-buton* and I was sitting next to him and Charlene was sitting in Eva's lap. We were at work on our third bottle of champagne. It was just dusk, the end of the summer, and there was that feel to the air that one season is passing too quickly into another. Later I would realize Lucy taught me that. At the time, I felt glad and serene and profoundly comforted that we four were together that warm, endless night. When Eva got up to change the record, she put on soft jazz with an oboe somewhere in it, but she didn't go back to Charlene. She sat down between Dan and me. There was paint on her fingers and she smelled of oleander. There was another bottle of champagne, and then Dan was gone. Maybe if he hadn't left, I don't know. Charlene had her hands around my ankles, and Eva had such a soft tongue.

Almost, I would like to tell you Lucy found us there, entwined as we eventually became, that she wept and made a scene, behaved badly. Or I'd like to say it never happened, that as soon as I realized Eva and Charlene were lovers and had been for months, I went home and went to bed by myself. I tell you I'm normal and I am, but normal depends on the circumstance and two soft tongues are more pleasure than any woman can resist. That being so, what I'd really like to tell you is that Lucy was gone by the morning, she just up and left us all on her own. But of course that isn't true either, and whatever I did, in any circumstance I'm telling this story and I still have some feeling for the truth. What happened is this: in the morning I went home and found Lucy waiting, eager to show me her weaving.

You could, when we got to her house, feel the absence of Charlene, but it wasn't heavy, the way I always thought. It was just she wasn't there. It was just a quiet morning in September.

"Dan was here last night," Lucy said.

I looked at her and I looked at her loom in the corner of the room and I felt, I don't know why, tiredness and something very close to dread.

"We had a long talk," she said when I said nothing. "It isn't easy for him."

"So tell me who it's easy for. Is it easy for you?"

Lucy took me by the hand and led me very gently across the room. Her own hand was warm and soft. I didn't want to look so I watched her face instead. Devoid of any sense of drama, it nonetheless reflected keen anticipation.

"Lucy, wait," I said.

She turned, surprised. "But I want you to see..."

"In a minute." And suddenly, possessed of an unexpected urgency, I knew what all that time I had been avoiding, not calling her, not coming over. Lucy lived her life directed by a certain knowledge, bordering on courage, and she asked too much of us with her suffering. Despite my own feeling of guilt, I wanted a confession. I wanted it before whatever she was weaving confirmed it. "First tell me what you talked about with Dan." My voice was clear and steady and I think I may have smiled.

Lucy sighed. "Oh you know, we talked over things. Plans. What we want. Dan was a little drunk, I think."

"Did that matter, that he was drunk?"

"No." Lucy seemed so calm. "We told the truth. We told each other how we feel. Dan was very insistent, and I think maybe I was too."

Now for an instant I wasn't sure, but I had started this thing and, maybe a little like Dan, I had to finish. "What did you tell him?" I said, thinking *Say disarmament, say children, lie if you have to but don't make this harder on us, on me.* The only thing is, Lucy is Lucy, and with absolute precision she went ahead and named not what I know now to have been throughout that time my own greatest desires, but uncannily, their opposite.

"Two things, really," she said. "I told him I want that my heart should never heal over. And I told him I want always to be loved."

Between us, then, we had at last come to the end of our lies, and so I turned to look at what she'd made and there was Charlene's sun just emerging. It was intricate and moving and very beautiful, and I was trying to think how to tell her when Lucy flipped the fabric to reveal Dan's solemn moon. This was not a trick, this was real: night and day, moon and sun, somehow she'd fused them together. Now she kept smiling and smiling.

"You know," she said, "I'm making it for you."

Even at the time I knew I could never have stopped her from saying so, but I wanted to, just as I wanted to stop myself from saying, "For me? But good lord, Lucy, how could you?"

And then she laughed, not so much as if it were funny but rather, it seemed, for the sound of the laughter, low and full and perfectly delighted. "It was easy." She was still smiling. "I'm normal. Aren't you?"

WELL I moved, but who I missed after I moved was not any of them but Mr. and Mrs. Johnson instead. And I missed the children we never had. Still, children not born remain useless regrets and Mr. and Mrs. Johnson were not at all like that. Whenever I pass our old block these days I think of how they couldn't look at us – him with his groceries, her with her cane – and how I couldn't look at them. I know, too, which church they attend and one Sunday I almost went looking for them, but I'm not old yet and there's forty years between me and that. In that much time I wonder if I'll come to understand what love is, or why I touch myself in this new way. I think they loved each other, Mr. and Mrs. small old Johnson, but all that seems unrelated to all this. Lucy must have finished her tapestry by now. It wasn't finished when I saw it, just enough to see what I saw. What I saw was that I had to move. The only thing left, I think, is this: in the back of my lingerie drawer I still have a scrap of green silk. I want to tie it up if I could just think where. At night I think: *Where*? I'm thinking it now. But there aren't any trees in my new apartment complex. And of course I'm still me and I can't even go to my lingerie drawer.

Natural Histories

I. GEOLOGY

Directions: To get to the desert, you must want to go there. Buy a map, study sand and the faces of Indians, and prepare as best you can for leaving the linear world and entering a circular one.

BRUNO is holding up a T-shirt with his name on the back and a color reproduction of a childhood photo in which, at age four, he grips the wrong end of a baseball bat and, dressed up for the majors, stands determined at home plate.

"I was four years old and my head was in my hands," he says.

"Bruno's family," Tillie says, "is obsessed with monograms."

Maja says, "Put it on," and Bruno pours more gin and tonic for everyone, as it is hot and the refrigeration in the motel doesn't work. Or it works too well, with a blast of icy air that smells faintly of dust and dead mice, so they leave it off. Every building on the reservation smells like that, and the three of them are getting tired of their tour. All day they have ridden

the Canyon de Chelly in giant jeeps Maja calls canyon mon-
sters. When the jeeps stopped, they took off their shoes and
waded through the warm river in quicksand that sucked to
their ankles, their knees. On the sheer walls above them,
eight-hundred-year-old handprints, still red as if etched in
blood, pressed sternly down. At one point, at a thick growth
of cottonwoods, just in front of a crude wood fence, a govern-
ment sign clearly read: NAVAJO FARM. Tillie saw a boy leading
some sheep. The next time they stopped, she lay down in the
river and let the water wash gently around her.

"The sand is like silk," she said. "Get down with me in it."

Huge purplish whorls marked the cliffs above them. Bruno
pulled her up and they rode on. Now, as if to apologize, he
puts on his T-shirt and says, "On the other hand, I've always
been very interested in the Bill Williams River."

Tillie makes a sharp, angry sound behind her teeth. "Have
you?" she says.

"I came to learn the desert," Maja says, intercepting them.
"You see, I write poems, but they're banal."

"I sell insurance," Bruno says. "You can't get much more
banal than that."

"But it's too complicated," Maja persists. "You don't ever
know which to prefer."

"Gin," Tillie says. "I always take gin, so that's easy."

"I mean about the ruins, or else the living canyon. I'm so
tired of making decisions, of intruding."

"What do you write about?" Tillie asks, a little coyly.

"Well, I'm working on a series now called *Drawings of Dead
Morticians.*"

There is a pause, and then Bruno says, "It's ironic. What I
do, I prepare my clients for disaster so it never seems that way.
Whereas I myself, in fact, prefer adventure."

BUT THEN theirs was never a gentle friendship, Bruno's and
Tillie's, from the word go. Better to wound than to caress, he

always said, and as Tillie did not know quite what to say to that, she said nothing. This she now attributes to two things: how when they met on a college geology trip, Bruno, seduced by the landscape, paid more attention to the jagged line of mountains at the horizon than he did to his magnifying glass, and the perfect fusion of her parents. It was the most amazing thing. Whenever her father received some award, her mother bought a new dress and fairly beamed for two weeks. If her mother wept, her father sat beside her (the weeping woman, not the child) and placed a large hand on her shoulder, and mumbled things Tillie never understood. What she did understand was that if human beings reproduced the same way as guinea pigs, they achieved love like snakes: out of an old skin when the time came, and into another, your lover's, forever, half him. Tillie never counted on the ego. Bruno, in the first bloom of their sexual relations, was just back from Alaska and talked off the cuff as if right out of books, but it was all show, bluff, self-conscious bravado. Tillie, beguiled, fell in love with his drifting. It was all the same to Bruno, but Tillie began to be concerned that they were squandering their twenties. Concern grew into alarm. She did her level best.

When Bruno had his plan to go to Mexico and build their own adobe, Tillie studied the properties of mud. He thought he might go to law school so over dinner, for as long as that lasted, she tried out her logic on him. Then he taught English to Asians and she practiced his drills.

"My mother likes football," he prompted, "you know."

"Just joking, of course," she said the response. "My father likes knitting."

"Here," Bruno told her, "my Taiwanese and Koreans burst into hysterical laughter."

Tillie imagined twenty dark happy faces. It's supposed to be funny, she thought. Then she said, "And the Vietnamese?"

"My cat likes swimming, you know," he said. Bruno was grim teaching humor.

Still, Tillie didn't give up. She couldn't, for she had abandoned her own skin in the first stunning weeks of their friendship; now, naked, raw, she needed another, and Bruno's was the only one that fit.

It went on. For three years she saved all their old toothbrushes in hopes that they really might go on an archaeological dig; she subscribed to several literary journals to inspire him to creativity; she clipped baseball box scores out of pure desperation. Bruno, obdurate, took off alone. Tillie got postcards from Israel, Africa, Spain. *I want you*, he wrote, *to suffer over something deeper than your not being beautiful.* Later he wrote: *The loudest sound of a frightened man is his cry at orgasm. I need a woman to complete my life.* He came home; they were married; and Tillie, vindicated, went right ahead and put rosemary back in her spaghetti sauce. She shivered with pleasure and daring. It was time, she concluded, that Bruno get respectable.

"Stop whining," Bruno said. "Don't nag."

"I'm not nagging," Tillie said. "Just choose a career."

This was in San Diego and though one hundred miles north the vicious Santa Ana winds were ravaging Los Angeles, in San Diego all was still. Shadows on the sidewalks were as if etched. Balls bounced on playgrounds echoed through countless condominium complexes. It was very hot. And Tillie was very proud of herself, for she was not thinking *love, transcendence*, as she had on that long-ago geology trip, she was thinking *house*, she was thinking *washing machine*, she was thinking she was leaving something out but she couldn't think what. Bruno got a job in social service, where he worked half time with alcoholics and the other half with juvenile delinquents.

"A hell of a way to make a living," Tillie said.

Bruno was transferred to abortions. Every night there was another girl, and all of them fifteen. Tillie started smoking. Bruno burned out. They were poor, they were married, and they wanted so much to get back at each other that when

Bruno finally quit, his new plan was insurance.

"You want stable?" he said. "I'll give you stable." And then he had one thousand business cards printed up.

Tillie took it as he meant it, not as a gesture of contempt or of spite, but of both. She was twenty-eight years old and had a vision of herself that wouldn't go away. In it she was six, wearing yellow pedal pushers and with her bangs tied up in a topknot. It was fall then, but still warm in the valley where she lived. She was sitting in the sun in the front of her house and digging at the dirt with a stick, and each time she dug, she thought of something else good about her life – the enormous blue butterflies on the walls of her bedroom, the way her father kissed her on the forehead when he tucked her in at night, how even if she had to eat peas she had good food to eat and plenty of it, that already she was six and she hadn't perished yet in any nuclear war, and with luck, she might live to have a boyfriend, go to college. After awhile, she put down the stick and placed her hand over her heart, which seemed to expand to embrace the world and felt full of tenderness and grace. She sat that way until her mother called her to dinner. Now she called Bruno to dinner and tried to tell him about it.

"Unlike what my mother told me about India," she said, "I had food at least, and a clean bed, and parents who loved both each other and me."

Bruno looked up something in a notebook, though the food was getting cold.

"And we weren't Russia either. Life was good."

Bruno called a client. By the time he was done, the clarified butter for the artichokes was hard and speckled with tiny yellow granules. Tillie got the mayonnaise. They ate in silence. When dinner was over Bruno said, "According to some rich Korean businessman I read about, it is better to decide than to make the right decision. Surely you can understand that."

That night a terrible longing rose up in Tillie from a depth not even she would ever have suspected. It came at the most unexpected moment. She was washing the dishes and the cup in her hand – sheer porcelain and, around and around the rim, hand-painted with yellow and purple flowers, irises, she thinks – was her grandmother's, and as she stared at it rinsed with light and water in her hand just then, the hand itself, as if imbued with a life of its own, became consumed with the desire to touch Tillie's grandmother's hair again, though the older woman had died ten years before. It was white hair from as long as Tillie knew it, and she had the palest of pale blue watery eyes. For Tillie at the moment it was as if something large and solid within her had suddenly shifted. She might even have given a slight cry. Eyes closed, she tried to remember her grandmother but all she could remember was her fine and silky hair, thinning in the months before her death. Bruno was reading claims in the bedroom. Tillie went to him and began to stroke his hair.

"What are you doing?" he said. "Get off."

"I love you," she said.

"Get off," he said. "I said get off."

This went on for awhile, six months perhaps. Bruno remained angry, vehement, alarmed. Tillie had no clear thought at all, but seemed to float through everything, passionate, insubstantial, as if the longing that took hold of her that night had replaced her very being, for soon it spread, touching everything, like a pulse or yet undisciplined love. The least provocation could set it off – the sound of a piano three houses down, spring quail foraging on a hillside, children. All the time she walked around with this longing a very nearly palpable thing inside her. Sometimes she could almost feel the throb of it lodge against her chest at the sight of a mauve-colored tulip, alone beside moss-covered steps to what once was a house where whole families lived out their destinies but was now a green vacant lot.

Tillie wept and waited and yet despite her isolation, what she felt was something strange and absolute, like the high sweet hiss of the wind, especially when they made love, so that even in waiting there was a kind of lushness and amazement. And she was not without hope. In small ways, at first, and then in larger, less mysterious ones – her noticing a poster of Greece, them watching the Russian ballet on TV – this thing that had entered now even her sleep and riddled every dream with a red boat, a thin man, a strange woman, slowly was forging itself into a plan, banal enough, but just, she thought, and also not impractical. When Bruno finally sold a large group policy, she tried out her idea of a vacation. He looked at her like she was crazy. She steeled herself for the duration.

This took stages and a definite method, beginning with the general principle and up to and including all the many, specific details – timetables, tickets, accommodations – and also Bruno's individual psychology. It was part of her strategy to let him veto Europe, South America, Hawaii. Then she went to work on the Caribbean, New Zealand. The issue stayed open. She went to travel agents and left colorful brochures scattered around the living room. It was getting to be spring and she could hear the girls playing hopscotch on the sidewalks, the boys tossing balls in the street. The scent of orange blossoms settled in the corners of every room and under their sheets at night. Tillie hated her washing machine.

Even so she was completely ill-prepared for how Bruno had his own plan, and for how, just when she had begun to despair, he mixed up a pitcher of dry martinis and picked up a random brochure. His voice was cool, professional, as he read out loud about southwestern tours, and it really did sound as though suddenly, perversely, he'd grown interested in the desert. Naturally it was calculated. The thought of a tour horrified Tillie.

"But a tour," she said. "This is supposed to be for us. And

besides, Arizona is practically home."

"We'll meet people," he said. "We need that."

"Old people," she said. "Assholes and goons."

Bruno remained deliberate and firm. "We need to meet people. That's all there is to it."

And Tillie, at last, gave in, for just to go somewhere was all that finally mattered: in her head, even the desert became imbued with tenderness and grace, and she imagined how the sky would turn at night and what animals would cry out beneath it.

WHEREAS Maja was very much the opposite of Tillie and when the man she spent her twenties with wanted to have children, she left him just like that, believing when the bombs dropped, there'd be no place for them. It was a true belief but a hard one to sustain, for people, Maja found, lacked tolerance, in general, and also courage for the end of everything. Thus, in her thirtieth year, Maja came to understand that she'd been wrong and that she was, after all, a bad person, because she'd traded form for content in her life. It had worked when she was younger, when form had seemed both beautiful and necessary, but even then, she realized now, it also worked to alienate her irrevocably from the man she was destined to love and live with forever. But destiny has its own purpose and after ten years began to operate by other laws than those she'd grown accustomed to relying on. Then she wanted them back again, every possibility she'd ever spurned because it was either less or different from what she had imagined. But it was a whole new world she had to deal with, and the men it seemed might lie within her destiny were married.

THESE, then, are our travelers, in whom there is both grief and a great deal of common experience. They all have college educations. They all prefer green vegetables to beef, *The Nation* to *Time,* and the pride of speaking out on what they think to the subtlety of perhaps not always knowing, of perhaps the world changing and them with it. You will maybe blame them, but you oughtn't, for they never blamed each other. And they know something about fate, these three, who were born the year the Rosenbergs were killed and who came into awareness when the San Francisco Giants lost the World Series. And then there was the Cuban missile crisis, and then, of course, the President was dead. Maja lowered the school flag to half mast; Tillie led a prayer; Bruno fainted. They were, each privately, preparing for the war and for the day their mothers would take off their flowered skirts and trade the wringer washer in on something automatic. Later Bruno would say to Tillie, "The world kept twisting an extra degree on its axis, just enough to throw us off and send us spinning." And Tillie would re-member how assassination followed assassination and end-less televised riots and once the taste of tear gas on her way to class, and she would run her hand down Bruno's chest and say, "Well, of course you had the draft then too. It was awful." Maja, with her own idiosyncrasies, charted the possible ends of the world against a line graph of their psychosexual develop-ment. This, too, was involved in why she left her lover.

Thus, Maja adjusted the way she could, in the same way Bruno sold his insurance, in the same way Tillie nurtured her unspeakable host of desires. There was nothing ideal about it, but even so they all had their private moments: Tillie once watched a train at night from the perfectly wild bank of a river, Maja was mugged, Bruno made love with a boy. What is sacred is sacred because it takes us out beyond the world and we must not forget it, for surely, as we surround ourselves with chil-dren, houses, obligations, the gap between how things might be and how they are becomes increasingly diminished and eventually negligible. All that is left, perhaps, is that youth seems a vaguely better time, from which, if we are so inclined, we retain a small handful of stories that, by repetition, come to seem a kind of icon, not less holy for its secular nature and just about as substantial as religious ecstasy.

For these reasons and others our travelers have come rather later in life to the breaking-off point and we are fortunate enough to have caught them on the cusp, finding them as we do in their early thirties and sprawled with self-conscious languor on the worn furniture of a reservation motel, designed western-style for tourists, assholes, and goons. With nothing to speak of to distinguish them, they fit right in, for certainly it is clear that at this particular moment they have not the slightest inclination toward heaven.

Bruno, for instance, who sells insurance, is just noticing that Maja is full-breasted and clever, if a little pink from the gin or their day in the canyon. Tillie can't help but be outraged. She is thinking of what he just said, his famous preference for adventure, all those lies. Whatever he had promised that way had so quickly faded into indirection. And here he is now, showing off his ridiculous T-shirt.

"My mother sent me this," he says. "My mother loves me very much."

"The family jewel," says Tillie. "Put it on."

They have another drink and it gets dark, though from where they are they do not hear the cry of a single animal. Each is a stranger to the others. As a result, they work themselves into a frenzy of gaiety. Bruno does a little jig. Maja says some poems. Tillie runs out into the night, calling back in a high voice, "Oh, let's skip the trading posts."

It is suddenly very quiet. Bruno looks at the backs of his hands and says, "And do what?"

In the instant before Maja answers they hear Tillie's voice

sail forth into the night, but not with words. Maja touches
Bruno's knee. "I myself," she says, "have always been very
interested in the Bisti Badlands."

II. ASTRONOMY

To find constellations: Don't let anyone tell you stories are about
language. Stories are about love, for love is everything, and so are
stories.

AND THEN of course I've had my hand in this. In my own
way, you might say, I have made these characters for you and
placed them together in what you may have surmised will
become an increasingly odd circumstance. You will further
have been right to have concluded that the circumstance is the
single variable. The people are just themselves, with their own
lives and not, as I've said, without fate.

Which is not to say it could not have turned out differently
had I just changed a few things around – put them on a raft,
maybe, and shot them down a canyon. There, without access
to land, obliged to navigate and paddle, confined together in
a tight and awkward space, surely they would have played a
different story out. But I chose to give them the desert, about
which they know nothing at all.

How easy it would be, then, for them to miscalculate the
looseness of sand on the road and, just at the apex of some
unexpected curve, spin crazily off into one of those gorgeous,
unrelinquishing dunes. Or perhaps they will simply misread
the map, get lost, and end up at some Navajo enclave. Maybe
Maja will have heard to stay in the car.

"You should stay in the car," perhaps she will say. "You
should stay where they can see you, and wait for them to
come."

But maybe she will have forgotten. Bruno will get out to ask for directions – only that, directions, not food, not shelter, not transportation. The only thing is, intrusion is intrusion, and there would be violence. In this way, you would have your disaster, but you would also have a story without love, a non-story.

In other words, do not expect disaster, any more than you might expect sheer elegance of language. I'm not in this for sentences but for our unlikely travelers, who with a little forbearance and faith may transcend the limitations of their personalities and enter history, if only for a moment. Ask Maja, who just as you know that Tillie and Bruno ineptly struggled through the seventies, you must know she herself had a mother, the same as you and I, and that when she discovered makeup at fifteen her mother washed it off and called her a slut.

"Slit, slot, slut," Maja said to herself. She covered herself with her hands, felt nothing, and contrived to believe that was all.

Years later and just weeks after she left her lover, Maja found herself in Tijuana remembering, as she will now all her life, what he said to her just before she got on the bus, his last words. "Forbearance," he had said. "You must learn to forbear."

Tijuana was hot, the streets thronging with merchants and tourists and vacant-eyed women with babies strapped front and back, their hands perpetually raised as if to God. Maja had come to buy brandy and coffee and odd, scented bath soaps shaped like turtles and goats, but her mind was on forbearance when out of the mob a legless beggar on a three-wheeled platform careened around a corner and knocked her down. For a short time she lay, confused, in his path while he butted at her with his head. No one paid any attention. Maja returned to San Diego without buying anything and first showered, then bathed with plain Ivory, then got drunk on California wine and tried to sleep the nightmare out but had to masturbate. This is not language: this is fact. Maja, eventually, did fall asleep, and she dreamed, but whether of the beggar or nuclear holocaust or even some lover I don't know about, I can't say. And if I were to tell you what I can say about that first lover and Maja, it would be too familiar: their desires, their anxieties, their sense of betrayal and loss, their separation. That story tells itself, though Maja might object, for Maja, who lived through it, lacks discretion, and will, and a sense of proportion. But what the hell, he's just as well left out of things. He read her poems, he loved her dance, he was entranced, but then he wanted children. Whereas with Tillie and Bruno, Maja goes into the desert.

III. ARCHAEOLOGY

What they are looking for: rocks, burial mounds, dinosaur bones. That sort of thing.

IN THE morning they buy a map, rent a car, and sail along the highway through the reservation in high spirits. They do not think to bring food or water. Instead, they bring beer and Maja's dope and take enough of each to make the country outside, densely forested with sage, piñon pine, and Ponderosa, seem exquisitely beautiful. Tillie reads the map: turn east, then north, then east, then west on progressively smaller roads; find the Bisti Church; the Badlands are not far off. They turn east, climb a pass, and descend to where it's flat, made murky with haze, and where there is nothing but cactus and rocks.

"Follow cacti," Maja says. "Always follow cacti."

They turn north, then east. The road turns to gravel. They follow cacti and have another beer.

"Are we crazy?" Tillie says. "Let's be crazy."

Bruno speeds up on the rocky road. "This isn't like selling insurance," he says.

A rodent chases them as the morning approaches noon. There are no shadows anywhere, though still they follow cacti. Each shares a single thought: unlike the canyon with its quicksand, there is nothing tender here. The beer is getting warm.

After awhile Tillie says that she thinks they're supposed to turn west before long. When they do, the road turns to dirt. By their calculations, there are still seven miles. They clock seven miles on the odometer. Out of the wilderness, a white adobe church rises, its pine cross bleached pale gold against the sky. Maja and Tillie peer at the squiggles on the map, congratulating themselves on having successfully navigated so many blue and black lines, and now just this series of thin gray dashes. Fate, they are certain, is on their side for the day.

The road dips down into a wash. Bruno scans the horizon for a snack bar, his stomach responding as conditioned by the hour. No one thinks to look for hogans; no one wants to ask directions. The wash becomes another wash, and then another, an endless series of pitted gullies with the road traversing them not really much of a road anymore. Grass grows thigh-high at the middle of ruts carved by four-wheel-drive vehicles. In the seventh wash, at last Bruno sees a small sandstone column and stops. For several hours they have seen, besides the rodent, no other living thing. Even at the church no priest had tended any garden. After Bruno turns the rented engine off, only the wind makes any sound. It is very hot and they do not know where they are, but they get out anyway.

Almost at once Maja squats, picking up a light gray rock shaped like a shell. Beside it, another rock reflects a mirror image of the first in a fluted depression at its center. Tillie finds another pair. Bruno points out that they are abundant.

"But what?" Tillie says. "I don't get it."

"Fossils," Bruno says, sounding knowing.

Maja matches up two rocks. "So what are badlands anyway?"

Bruno, still standing, surveys the horizon. Nothing in his life has ever seemed so bleak. Even the cacti have disappeared and all the earth is dull tan or ochre, when at least he'd expected extravagant reds. He shrugs. "Badly eroded rock," he says, "with no soil."

BRUNO is very excited about the dinosaur bones. First he finds them in a sandstone hillside, then he calls and calls to the other two. Tillie is hot and as she responds slowly, so does Maja, not even remembering the uneven slant of Bruno's shoulders, not even thinking to keep these allegiances casual. When they come to the hill, it looks like rocks to them.

"Beloved husband," Tillie says, "you're thirty-one years old and your head's still in your hands."

Bruno brushes sand from an enormous clavicle, and Maja feels the sun descend into her knees. She squats, getting closer to the earth, but it isn't close enough. Bruno keeps digging and digging. He uncovers ribs. He uncovers a sternum.

"This is illusion," Tillie says. "This is your fantasy."

Maja stares, but says nothing. In the glare she might be crying. But Tillie is not without terror either before the two worlds, ancient and new, and after awhile the two women find shade in a perfectly uninteresting wash where they sit on flat, dun-colored rocks and stare disconsolately at the low opposite wall. The shade is only slightly cooler than the sun. Not far away, though they cannot see him, Bruno keeps uncovering what he believes are the remains of extinct animals. Tillie feels something stir inside her. Maja wants to leave this place, go far away, but it's too hot. She wants at least to have some dope, but it's in the car. She wants to say something to Tillie so she says, "Because we were never married, there was no necessity for divorce."

"Why were you afraid back there?" Tillie says, as if in answer.

"Who me?" Maja says. "I'm always afraid. You know, of the regular sorts of things – leaving my stove on, nuclear holocaust. But as I say, with us it was easy. He wanted a kid, so I split."

Tillie nods, more to herself. Maja is remembering four years of aimless wandering, of confusion, chaos, bad feelings, of pain, and mostly of distance. In the wash there are not even insects. Whatever caused it is no more.

"Four years ago," Maja says.

"Did you love him?" Tillie says.

"I loved him."

"Have you been in love since?"

For a long time, surrounded by so much dust and rock, Maja says nothing, but her hands open loosely on her knees. There is nothing she would give the world for and, at the moment, no reason especially not to. It is between weeping and talking.

"Do you want the truth?" she finally says. "I am afraid of my own bones, of the history they'll tell. And then of course I'm afraid they'll lie alone."

Tillie smiles, a little grimly, and leans languidly back against the dirt wall of their refuge. Maja looks away and leans back too. Where their feet extend before them, the sun circumscribes a bleak circle. Each retreats into her own reverie of sadness, without focus but yet not without substance. Maja, having said her piece, has nothing more to say. Tillie is remembering the handprints on the cliff wall they saw yesterday. She had marveled at how small they were, at how far up the cliff. When the Navajo walked by with his sheep, Bruno pointed up and said to Maja, "See those red marks there? Five hundred years ago an Indian, like him, placed his hand against that wall."

Maja had lifted her hair off her neck and said, "I wonder how they climbed so high."

"The floor of the canyon is lower now than then," Bruno told her.

Tillie, in her frustration, had said nothing, but in her heart she had cried out: *How much lower, don't you know, how fast do rivers cut?* Now she thinks more calmly about the slice of water through all those thousands of years. She thinks of the miracle by which that place alone preserved its sacred river, while here and for so many miles all around, just nothing.

Both women are nearly asleep when Bruno comes striding up the gully with a rock shaped like a small skull in his hands.

THEY follow the gully until it broadens to a flat, hard surface, like the dried bottom on a pond, riddled with intricate fissures and, in places, ruptured blisters. To the west there is an odd circle of stones, once piled chest high and now crumbling. Where mud had filled the gaps between, sun comes through now. Ahead, everything is white and dusty. Maja follows a deep crevice forward, motioning to Tillie and Bruno to follow, but Tillie turns instead toward the stones. Bruno calls out to her and then, in anger, to Maja. When neither makes any answer, he moves as if to go after Maja and then stops, half turning toward his wife.

"This is the desert," he says in a voice not loud, but just loud enough to be heard by both women.

"That's a hogan," Maja answers. "Someone died there, don't you see?"

"But we must stick together. We must not separate."

Tillie, having come to the structure of stones, places her hand on the outside wall. Maja is already nearing the cliffs at the far side of the flat. Bruno feels that things are suddenly out of his control and drops his skull-shaped rock in order to retrieve his wife, but by the time he has crossed the distance between himself and her, she is smiling in a way he has never seen before.

"Look," she says, "this is an entrance."

"What's going on?" he says.

"Do you think she's beautiful?" Tillie says.

"Who, Maja? I think she's full-breasted and clever."

Beyond them Maja disappears into the cliffs.

"You brought us here," says Tillie. "You rented the car and you drove us here. You say we need people. Go after her, Bruno."

She stands outside the entrance and looks first at Bruno and then toward the center of the stones. She is still smiling. Bruno says again that they must not lose each other.

"I've been saying that for years," Tillie says. "What are you afraid of?"

"That we'll get lost," Bruno says. "That we haven't any water. That night will come, and that it will get cold."

"That's what I mean," Tillie says. "Find Maja. I'll catch up with you later."

But when she turns to enter the peculiar structure, Bruno catches her arm and will not let her go. In that instant, despite their endless years of marriage, they are more strangers to each other than ever, red-faced from the heat and damp with sweat. Above them the sky turns a deeper shade of blue. Bruno, who wants very much to kiss that spot on Tillie's neck that pools the perspiration he can almost, looking at it, taste, has already forgotten about his fossils.

"Do you remember that field geology trip?" he says.

"You were seduced by the landscape," Tillie says.

"That's a lie. I was seduced by you."

Tillie laughs, not unaffectionately, but not as if she believes him either. Bruno wants to say *Believe me,* though he knows now he cannot ask that much. The shadow of a hawk circles once around them. Tillie smiles in that new way again. It would be so easy to forgive him one more time. Instinct alone preserves her.

"You asked," Bruno says when the moment has passed. "I'm afraid of the future."

"I know."

"And of love."

THE NATURE of landscape is not at all metaphorical. This is difficult for us, as we have passed beyond a decent sense of grace and must rely on intellect, however feeble. And certainly there are mythologies for every land, especially the desert: ancient seabeds, handcuffs and birdcages, the circular world, you name it. But mythologies aside, there is the earth itself, harsh, dry, unrelenting, and composed of the most unimaginable colors. You can find aqua there, among the deep reds (and here I must say that, earlier, Bruno had not yet looked closely enough), and lavender, and green, and every shade of yellow, light for artists. You can also find the most perfect white, all color, or absence of all color, I can't ever remember. Cacti bloom. Water takes on a different significance. The sky, in its sometimes blueness, sometimes opalescent translucence, ceases even to resemble its own self. So yes, we can talk circles, but we must also talk rocks. We must ask ourselves the question: *What are we to do with all these rocks?* Or again, we may talk, as Maja might have more openly to Tillie (*Yes, I loved him. But he was so far away, no matter when we even lived together. And when the world ends we won't be any closer. That's what I'm afraid of, how far away we'll be when the world ends, and how, whether it's thousands of miles or just the next room, we'll die with so much distance in between us, and all because I wouldn't have a child to have it die alone in so much distance. So here we are among the dinosaurs.*

I'd rather not have known any of this. Would you?) of annihilation and the death of everything.

But Maja looks at things in her own way and because of how she feels is afraid of a certain kind of beauty, as much the beginning as the end. The thing is to find the beauty as it presents itself to us and to succumb to it. It's the succumbing we resist, for the desert is eternal. I don't mean to be vague or even mystical. I do, however, want to suggest that there is deference, worship, if you will, and that in things eternal we may somehow move beyond our own fear, and with it, the perhaps not inevitable horror of Maja's vision, the big bang, nuclear holocaust, distance. Which, finally, is all I ever meant about love in the first place.

BRUNO finds Maja in a small, dark amphitheater halfway up the cliff. In one hand, she holds a smooth cylinder of striped gold petrified wood; in the other, fine red sand. He has had to scramble up vertical jumbles of rocks, through narrow crevices. His right knee and his left palm bleed. He is panting and forlorn and has no thought at all but to set the world back on its true course, if he can, if he knows how.

"This," he says when he catches his breath, "is one of the most interesting places I've ever been."

"It isn't even Bisti," Maja says. "Sit down." She shows him the rock. She scatters the sand. She touches his knee just below where he scraped it. "So," she says in a low voice, "Tillie is still with the ancestors."

"A lot you know," says Bruno. "Have you ever been in love?"

Maja looks at him as if he has just spoken in tongues. "What does that have to do with it?"

Bruno brushes the red sand into a pile, scatters it, brushes it up again, staring out at the barren wilderness below, the circle of stones where, if he could see inside, Tillie sleeps now. They have turned another degree into the late afternoon, and the heat has transformed the sky from its previous blue to that other translucence, more milky, like the surface of quartz or an egg. Despite himself, Bruno feels as if, if he could swim through it, he would take great gulps that would taste somehow like his own mother's milk, what Tillie's milk will be like if she's willing. Bruno makes a gesture toward something beyond them and thinks if he could only just imagine a taste close to that taste, suddenly, miraculously, he would be able to explain to this strange, full-breasted woman why love has everything to do with it.

But Maja has her own history and no argument concerning Tillie's once frail voluptuousness will ever convince her that Bruno has failed and betrayed his wife because there was a war, or because they grew into adulthood on the cusp, but because, and Maja knows this, Bruno felt clumsy and dangerous in bed. So when he bends to kiss the inside of her knee, she takes it as he means it – a blessing, a trial, a curse, and salvation. The heat of the day finally enters their bones and together they turn toward the sun. It is all they can do, for they are sick of words that describe what they're afraid of – of Maja's bones, of Tillie's not having children, of things ending here and like this, without birth and rebirth, discovery and rediscovery, without rocks preserved from the beginning to whatever in the world is coming next.

BELOW, when Tillie wakes, it is not that her grandmother has come to her in a dream, kissed her forehead, and let her feel her hair. Nothing at all like that has happened, in part because whoever's hogan it was is no ancestor of Tillie, and in part because Tillie's grandmother has very little to do with anything. She lived and died in a different world and Tillie, in fact, can barely remember even her fine, silky hair just now, for in her sleep she has emptied herself of her own thought, turned once, and waked. Awake, she simply goes outside again, into the shadows of the last of the day. Hers, which she decides to follow, is longer than she has ever seen it. What was white is gray, and all the reds are turning purple. Because she is thirsty, she finds a small green stone and places it underneath her tongue. She walks quietly. In her head she knows how she will find them, not touching, but having touched. In her heart she is grateful to them both. For so many years Tillie has conceived of herself as having things happen to her. Now she knows that she has been spared. And no, she does not think *children*, she does not think *What will happen*? If she thinks, as she walks, anything at all, she thinks how maybe later tonight, maybe when they get home, she will turn to Bruno in their bed and gather him up in her arms this new way. And she thinks how when she does, somewhere far away, Maja will turn in her sleep.

But you know that isn't exactly it either. I have told you Tillie's end, but Tillie's only one of three and there are possibilities even I have not considered. Bruno may not know what hit him. Maja may have powers to elicit the full grace of forgiveness. She has that larger side to her, as well as that troubling gap her barrenness, these past four years, has come to be. Or I could make it very bad for them, in such a hostile universe and without water.

But I also have this image in my head of them sailing back along the highway through the dark. In the rear seat Maja dozes, waking off and on to trace the path of a full and luminous moon. In the front, Bruno and Tillie chat as married couples do, wondering if the neighborhood boy has remembered to water the herb garden too, deciding that when they get back they will go to their favorite Mexican restaurant and drink Margaritas until someone asks them to leave. No one feels alone anymore. Everyone is content. They arrive safely back at the motel to find the others blandly playing cribbage.

But no, there is silence in the car and a feeling of suspension, like a dream or the presence of the spirits they've disturbed. After awhile they come to a dune they have never seen before, high and white against the night sky and casting the blackest shadow. "Like the light side, the dark side," someone says, "of the moon." It is instinct for them to get out and climb, for from the top of this dune anything may happen: Tillie may leave Bruno; Maja may decide to go back to her lover; they may all three lie together in an embrace which may last, as we understand time, forever, or from which instead such conceptions will occur. How pretty they look in this light. How soft the still warm sand against their bodies is as they sink down into it and release a common sigh.

It is all possible, every word of it, and what you want is that I should tell you, but I won't. The only true thing is that this is the desert. And Tillie has just awakened alone somewhere toward the far end of the afternoon. Because it is desert, there won't be much dusk. It will be light and then it will be dark, with no more shadows, just like that. So what the hell, she picks up a couple more of those stones – smooth, round, pink ones – and tries to sight the others on the cliff. She shades her eyes against the oblique slant of the sun. She lifts her hand still higher up in what might, from a distance, seem a wave. And is that where all this ends, with her looking up and them looking down, watching her finger small stones for them to put under their tongues like her? Well, yes. With that, and with the sense that whatever configuration I leave these people in, they remain terrifically small in this landscape. You must therefore look very closely and pay the strictest attention: Tillie smiles to herself in her new way, and just at this instant, Bruno moves as if to stand and call out to her.